When You Were Here

ALSO BY DAISY WHITNEY

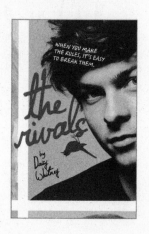

When You Were Here

DAISY WHITNEY

LITTLE, BROWN AND COMPANY
New York · Boston

Little, Brown and Company

Hachette Book Group
237 Park Avenue, New York, NY 10017
Visit our website at lb-teens.com

Little, Brown and Company is a division of Hachette Book Group, Inc.
The Little, Brown name and logo are trademarks of Hachette Book Group, Inc.

The publisher is not responsible for websites (or their content) that are not owned by the publisher.

First Paperback Edition: June 2014
First published in hardcover in June 2013 by Little, Brown and Company

Library of Congress Cataloging-in-Publication Data

Whitney, Daisy.
When you were here / by Daisy Whitney. — First edition.
pages cm
Summary: When his mother dies three weeks before his high school graduation, Danny goes to Tokyo, where his mother had been going for cancer treatments, to learn about the city his mother loved and, with the help of his friends, come to terms with her death.
ISBN 978-0-316-20974-8 (hc)—ISBN 978-0-316-20975-5 (pb)
[1. Grief—Fiction. 2. Cancer—Fiction. 3. Mothers and sons—Fiction. 4. Tokyo (Japan)—Fiction. 5. Japan—Fiction.] I. Title.
PZ7.W6142Wh 2013   [Fic]—dc23   2012031409

10 9 8 7 6 5 4 3 2 1

RRD-C

Printed in the United States of America

This book is dedicated to my parents,
who have given me so much love.

This story was inspired by the beautiful life
of Sharon Schneider, who showed her family
the world, and how to live.

Chapter One

When someone you love has died, there is a certain grace period during which you can get away with murder. Not literal murder, but pretty much anything else.

So I'm leaving the school parking lot on the second to last day of my senior year, and I'm driving down Montana Avenue, and this red Mazda Miata cuts me off.

I ignore the Miata. But a few blocks later, I turn onto my street and notice a silver Nissan. No one's in it; the car is just parked on the side of the road, hanging maybe a few inches into my driveway, and I have nothing against this car, or against the car's owner, but I am tired of everyone being gone, and I am tired of everything that has tired me out for the last five years of my life. Besides, when making decisions, my mom always said: *At the end of my life, when*

I'm looking back, will I regret not doing this? Fine, she was usually talking about traveling to Italy or taking me out of school to surf one afternoon. Still, I'm pretty sure I'm *not* going to regret hitting this car for no reason, so I bang into it one, two, three, four, five, six times, each hit radiating under my skin, jump-starting me like paddles to shock the system.

It works for a few seconds. I feel a spark inside me, like a match has been lit in a darkened cave. But then it's snuffed out and I'm back to the way I was before.

I shift into reverse, and my car's fender makes this annoying scratching sound as it drags against the road. I pull into my driveway, and I get out of my car. I walk around to the front, and the fender is dangling down to the ground, and it looks like the engine might be smoking, but I don't feel like dealing because dealing requires too much energy, and energy is what I lack. I head inside, toss the keys on the table by the door, and flop down onto the couch.

My dog, Sandy Koufax, joins me, curling up with her head on my knee. As I rub Sandy Koufax's ears, I wonder briefly if they will send me to anger-management class or something, but there's no *they* to send me away. Sure, there's Kate, my mom's best friend, but she won't. The other *they*s are all gone. My mom died two months ago, my dad was killed in an accident six years ago, and my sister, Laini, is in China trying to rediscover her roots, something I don't get, but then again I don't get a lot about my sister because we don't have a lot in common, least of all genes.

She is adopted from China, and I am *a white boy*, as she likes to say when she deigns to speak to me.

I put my arms behind my head and consider—what else can I get away with? Is there a statute of limitations on how long you can have a free pass after your mom dies? Because smashing that car is the only thing that's made me *feel* in weeks.

I glance at the empty pizza box on the coffee table and pull it toward me with my foot to see if there might still be a slice in it. I notice Sandy Koufax watching my foot, then the box.

"Sandy Koufax, did you finish the pizza?"

She says nothing. Just tilts her sleek black head to the side.

"Well, can you call and order another one?"

She puts one of her white paws on my chest.

The phone rings. I stretch out my arm over to the coffee table, grab the phone, and answer. Mrs. Callahan from next door wants to know if I am all right. *No, I am not all right*, I want to say. *Have you been to my house? Have you seen how empty it is?*

"Yup," I tell her as I flip through the mail: some notices from UCLA, where I'm going in the fall, a bill from Terra Linda High about the cost of my cap and gown. I have to give the valedictory speech in a few days. I toss that envelope away. It crash-lands on the cool, white tiles on the other side of the coffee table where I can't see it anymore. Looking at it reminds me of what's missing from graduation.

Because my graduation was *the one thing* my mom wanted most to see. It was her carrot, the thing she was holding on for. *I will be there, and I will take pictures, and I will be cheering and crying, and it'll be my last hurrah.*

Mrs. Callahan asks more questions about the *accident*, as she calls it. Not once does she say it was my fault. Not once does she ask if I rammed my car into another car.

"Do you need anything?" she asks.

A mom. A dad. Someone. Anyone. Can you arrange for that?

"Nah, I'm good."

Thirty minutes later Kate comes by. I know it's her from the repeated banging—her signature lately. Who says the Internet is changing how we communicate? We don't need the Internet. We have a town crier right here in Santa Monica, and her name is Mrs. Callahan—she must have told Kate.

I open the door for Kate, and she is pissed. I guess my statute of limitations has run out with her.

"I know you hit that car on purpose, Danny," she says, and her voice is loud. She is supposed to be my surrogate mom now or something. She played that role a few times the last couple years, like when my mom was at one of her treatments. My mom wasn't down for the count often, though. She was tough; she tried hard to get well. You don't hang on for five years unless you want to live. She wanted to live so badly, she visited Mexico and Greece and Japan many times, seeking out Western doctors and then Eastern medicine and then anything to try to live. But she came up two months short of her goal. Sixty lousy days. Kate's her best friend and has been since they went to college together. Kate also happens to be the mother of the girl I lost my virginity to. The girl who was mine for three perfect months last summer, and who then left my life without a reason, with barely a call.

Holland.

The most incredible and the most vexing person I know. It is unspoken, but deeply understood, that Kate and I don't discuss her daughter. If we were to talk about Holland, I'd never be able to talk to Kate about anything else.

I shrug. "So?"

"Why did you hit a car on purpose, Danny?"

Kate is a tiny person. She's maybe five feet tall, but she's a pit bull, and the muscles on her arms are sick. She works out every day, which is not unusual in Los Angeles, granted, but it's where she works out that's telling. She works out at Animal House, which is this very macho, very old, very broken-down gym without air-conditioning. The clientele is mostly Arnold Wannabes and guys just out of jail.

"I don't know." I walk to the sliding-glass door and open it. Kate follows me. Sandy Koufax does too, then noses a Frisbee on the grass. I pick it up. It has teeth marks etched along the surface. It's purple and says FIGHT CANCER. A lot of good that did. I throw it far into the yard, around the edge of the pool. Sandy Koufax is like a rocket—she chases it, catches up to it, leaps and grabs.

This dog might be the definition of perfect.

"So you did hit it on purpose?"

"Define *on purpose*."

"With intention," she says crisply.

"Yes, then. I did."

"What would your mother think?"

I throw the purple disk to Sandy Koufax again. She executes another excellent catch.

"Hard to say," I answer. "But let's be honest. She was never a big car person. She always said walking was healthier, so maybe she'd have been glad."

Kate narrows her eyes. "Not funny."

"But true. It is true," I add, and Kate doesn't answer because she knows how my mom felt about cars. My mom was one of the few people in LA who walked anywhere. I toss the Frisbee again. Sandy Koufax leaps, easily clearing three feet on the vertical. "Sweet! Did you see that, Kate? That is one fine dog."

I'll have to see if UCLA will let me have a dog in my dorm. Maybe I'll get an *orphan exception*.

Kate holds out her hands. "What am I supposed to do with you?"

I don't answer. There is no answer.

"Fine," Kate says, giving in. Her voice softens. "Just give me the insurance info. Give me the name of the claims adjuster, and I'll make sure everything is taken care of."

Kate is kind of like a wizard. Give her a shirt with a grease stain from last year. She'll get it out. Give her a pair of broken eyeglasses. She'll come back with a new pair free of charge because she'll convince the store it was owed to her. I give her my insurance info, and I know, in a day or two, this will all be taken care of. She's the fixer, and she likes it like that.

Her jaw is no longer set hard; her eyes are no longer narrowed. I'm in the clear. "Hey, Kate. Can you also call UCLA and see if I can bring a dog with me in the fall? If they allow that?"

"Of course. We'll get that dog on campus, no problem," she says, the look in her eyes softening as she reaches up to give me a kiss on the forehead. I let her, then I throw the Frisbee again to Sandy Koufax, and then again, and then one more time, and at some point Kate leaves, she may even hug me, she may even tell me she loves me, she may even say she's sorry that life sucks, but I'm lost in the throwing.

And then I realize I've been out here for hours. Because suddenly Sandy Koufax is exhausted. She jumps in the pool and starts paddling. I look up at the sun. When did it get to be so low in the sky? How did it become six in the evening when it was three just a few minutes ago?

I might as well join my dog, so I walk straight into the pool, cargo shorts, gray T-shirt, flip-flops, and all.

It's something, at least, the feeling of water sloshing all around me. I dunk my head, sinking under it all, then I come up and tell Sandy Koufax all the things I wish were different right now.

Chapter Two

Jeremy is shooting aliens, Ethan is trying to convince Piper that an earthquake of 9.0 magnitude will hit Los Angeles in the next 365 days, and half the girls volleyball team is schooling half the guys baseball team in pool volleyball. My former teammates are in the deep end on the other side of the net, getting clobbered by the bikini-clad athletes.

I turn up the volume on the sound system because Retractable Eyes is up next on the playlist, and this band is awesome. But before the opening chords sound, I hear the beginning of "Great Balls of Fire."

On. The. Piano.

I turn to the living room, and the aliens must have extinguished Jeremy because now he's leaning over the piano and he's thinking he's Jerry Lee Lewis.

"Dude, don't touch that." I walk over and stand next to the keys.

He pauses. "Just let me play this one song."

I shake my head. He knows this is my *one* rule. "Don't."

He pounds on more notes, and he's about to hit the chorus and to sing it too, belt it out, and I'm so not okay with this on so many levels because this is my mom's piano. She wasn't some classical performer or piano teacher or anything. But she liked playing for fun, banging out a show tune now and then or a Cole Porter number. Crossword puzzles, gardening, and a few old standards on the piano— those were her *little things in life*, the little things she did, the little things that made her happy.

"Jer. Off."

Something in my voice stops him, so he backs off, holds up his hands. "Sorry, bud."

"Go get one of Laini's guitars if you want to play something," I say, easing up a bit on my best friend.

"I wish you'd let me have it. You know you're never going to use the piano."

Jeremy's been on this music kick in the last three years. He's convinced that learning to play piano, guitar, drums, whatever, is going to help him with the ladies. I've seen no evidence of improvement in his scorecard with the opposite sex, but he can play the chorus from pretty much any top-ten most-downloaded tune of the moment. Maybe someday that skill will amount to something. For now, it's entertainment. And for now, and for forever, the piano's not for sale.

I remind him of that as he takes off for Laini's mausoleum of a room.

I survey the scene in my yard. Trevor, the lunking first baseman who I threw bunted balls to for the first three years of high school, smacks a volleyball in Cassie's direction. She tries to spike it back but hits air instead, and the ball skips out of the pool. She jumps out to grab it. She has the smallest bathing suit on, and she's also the weakest player on the team. Trina comes up behind me and whispers in my ear. "I see you watching her," Trina says as she runs a finger down my arm. What she doesn't say is, *I see you watching her and I don't care*, because, like me, there is little Trina actually cares about, least of all whether I check out other girls, even though I'm not checking out Cassie. If I were checking out girls, I'd only have eyes for one girl.

The incredible and vexing one who's not here, even though the lasagna she made me the other day is still in my fridge.

Trina trails her index finger across my palm, then adds, "Kicking in for you?"

"Starting to."

Trina brings me goodies too, only hers work better than food. She flashes a knowing grin, and I watch as she disappears into the kitchen, wearing low-rise jean shorts and a tank top that shows off her brown skin.

Jeremy returns with my sister's most expensive classical guitar. Laini played until eighth grade and was pretty damn good, so good my parents were thinking of sending her to some expert teacher at UCLA for lessons. But as with all things remotely American, Laini decided she wanted nothing to do with it. A guitar, even classical guitar, was the most American of all instruments, so she quit. A few years later she quit us too. Laini was never around when my mom became sick. Fine, Laini was in college already, had been for a year before the diagnosis, but she didn't even come home for the summer or for breaks, except for maybe one week a year. She was gone at the worst possible time, and as far as I'm concerned, that's the same as treating our mom like dirt. Suddenly I no longer want to hear her guitar. I want to *destroy* her guitar. I'm like a zombie, a living, breathing zombie who won't stop as I clunk toward Jeremy, who's jamming on my sister's handmade Tortorici guitar that my parents special-ordered for her twelfth birthday, and I yank it out of his hands right before he slides into a howling riff.

"I was just getting to the chorus."

"Go get another one and join me," I say, because Laini has more acoustic guitars in her unused room. "Are you in or out?"

"What are you talking about?"

I tip my head to the yard and mimic smashing a guitar.

He points to the Tortorici. "You know you can get a couple thousand on eBay for that."

I don't need the money. My mom saved well and invested well. We don't even have a mortgage anymore because she bought this house for cash when she sold off her last business a couple months before she was diagnosed. But not everyone is so *lucky* to have come into his parents' possessions at the tender age of eighteen. Or to have to figure out what to do with everything, from the property to the personal effects. Like her clothes. Her books. Her wigs.

I relent. "Take this one and do whatever you want with it. But get the others."

He thanks me, tucks the Tortorici under his arm, and races back up the stairs. Seconds later he's joining me in the yard, stumbling through the open sliding-glass door with a guitar in each hand, a pair of soon-to-be victims. He's followed by Ethan, Piper, and Trina, and we're all at the edge of the grass where a low rock wall hems in my yard.

I lift an ordinary wooden guitar high over my head, then nod at Jeremy. He can play master of ceremonies better than I can.

"It's not the end of high school until someone smashes a guitar," he shouts, holding his arms up in a victory sign. "That's a very famous saying, you know." Then to me, "The floor is yours."

I proceed to whack the living daylights out of the guitar to the encouraging cheers of my fellow classmates. Jeremy and Ethan join in, and even Piper bashes an old, cheap acoustic against the rocks. Trina jumps into action, her hazel eyes alive with the prospect of destruction, because Trina was a wild child in high school, and a wilder child in college and medical school too, and an even wilder adult now that she is smack-dab in the middle of her residency.

As I look down at the destruction—wooden shards everywhere, strings popped loose and languishing—I feel a trickle of endorphins, not like I just struck out the side but like I lobbed one good curveball. It's a lift, a momentary, temporary lift, a rising above this hazy line I've been living on.

But the problem is it's not enough to blot this all out, to quiet the whole wide world. It's not enough to bring back the sounds of Cole Porter being played, or flowers being planted, or of requests for a five-letter word starting with *A* or *T* or *C* or anything. Nothing is ever enough. Except Holland, who's tattooed all over me, but who's not here where I want her. I walk away from the carnage and return to the house. Trina follows, all lithe and pantherlike as she pads across the hardwood floors in her bare feet.

"Let's go to your room," she whispers in my ear.

I nod, take her hand, and lead her up the stairs. I hear the noises from outside, the splashing and the laughing, the sounds of cans opening and voices rising in the celebratory din of the end of an era, and then it fades when I close my door, crank up some tunes, and turn off the lights, leaving on a lamp by the side of my bed. Trina already has her top off, and she's pulling off my T-shirt, and the room's feeling fuzzy and warm, just the way I like it, because Dr. Trina gave me some new pills to try tonight. They've kicked in for me, and maybe for her, and everything, *everything*, just feels better when you're doing it on PKs.

She's already pinned me, my arms stretched above my

head, her hands on my wrists, her black hair falling all around my face. I'm never on top with Trina, but that's okay. She likes it this way, and it's easier, and she's never not hot. She's always ready, she's always racing, and she's always got her hands all over, and it's great, really, it's great.

Even though she's not Holland.

I curse silently.

I'd like to not think about Holland when I'm with someone else. I'd like to not picture Holland—her wavy blond hair, her sky-blue eyes, her lips tasting like strawberry, her smell—all girl, all pure, perfect, blond California girl.

But I can't *not* picture Holland.

So I close my eyes and go with it, imagining it's Holland holding me down. And it feels fantastic like that with imaginary Holland. It feels like I'm alive again, like I'm real again, like the earth is rotating around the sun again.

Then we're done, and Trina conks out in thirty seconds flat. Her face is pressed against my sheet; she doesn't even make it to a pillow. I watch her doze for a minute. Sometimes I think with every breath her brain is releasing all the X-rays and EKGs and patient reports she had to keep in her head all day. Sometimes I imagine her waking up next to a sea of warped, distorted readouts that have sort of melted out of her.

A strand of her long hair falls over her mouth. Her lips flutter while she's sleeping, trying to blow the hair away. I adjust her hair for her, tucking the strand behind her ear. Then I nod off too, not thinking about the people outside or the broken guitars. When I wake up in the middle of the night, my dog is wedged against me, and Trina is gone. But the good doctor has left something for me.

A fresh orange bottle of pills on my nightstand.

I'll need them to get through my graduation tomorrow. My mom was supposed to be in the front row.

Chapter Three

I always imagined that the morning before graduation would pass by in a blur of noise and barked orders. *Did you remember this? Did you forget that? Fix your hair; it's a mess.*

Like when Laini graduated. My dad grabbing his camera, my mom making sure Laini's cap was on right, me calculating how long I'd have to wear the striped polo shirt with the collar.

Now, as I pull on shorts and a T-shirt since it doesn't matter what you wear under the *robe*—because I refuse to call it a *gown*—the only sound I hear comes from Sandy Koufax, from her nails clicking against the floor as she switches locations, shifting from her early-morning yard patrol to her late-morning lounge-around-on-the-couch relaxation.

We didn't even have Sandy Koufax six years ago when

we raced out of the house for Laini's graduation, the last time we were all together—my mom, my dad, my sister, and me. That evening we went out to dinner in Chinatown at a restaurant Laini had researched because it had the best traditional Chinese dumplings, she said. She had already started down the path of reconnecting with her roots, so she ordered for all of us in Chinese too because she'd been studying the language.

"That's my girl," my dad said, then planted a kiss on Laini's forehead. She pretended to be cool and aloof, but she leaned into him, then responded in Chinese, and he laughed, then said something back. He had learned Chinese over the years, had taken classes, listened to Chinese podcasts, and had all the Learn Mandarin CDs in his car. My mom and I didn't know a word.

When the food arrived, my mom held up her glass and offered a toast. "To my daughter. I couldn't be more proud."

Then my dad. "To more education, which is Latin for ... *more bills*."

"Sorry I didn't get a scholarship," Laini said, and my dad immediately corrected himself. He never wanted Laini to feel bad about anything—fight with a friend, crummy grade, crappy haircut. Whatever it was, he'd save the day for her, even if he was the one who'd been sarcastic.

"I'm just kidding," he said. "Of course we've got the money."

"I'll go to state school," I offered, my contribution to the conversation.

"You're such a suck-up," Laini said to me.

My mom held out her hands. "Enough. Can we just have a nice dinner out?"

"How about a redo?" my dad said, and held up his glass. "To Laini Kellerman, who we are happily sending to college."

"Much better," my mom said, and nodded.

Laini held up her Coke and offered a toast. "To the end of an era."

Laini turned out to be a fortune-teller. A month later my dad was killed when he was hit by a truck in Kyoto. A year later my mom was diagnosed with cancer. Six years later, Laini doesn't even send me a graduation card.

My doorbell rings, and Sandy Koufax erupts in a flurry of barks from her post on the couch. When I answer the door, Holland's there. I tell myself to be stoic, especially since she's still wearing that star ring I gave her last summer. I hunted it down for her at a funky little clothing store on Melrose Avenue, since I knew that's where Holland liked to shop, where she loved to pick up cheap, little plastic bracelets and other jewelry.

"What?" She puts her hands on her hips and gives me a playful look as if I should have remembered she was going to be here. Fact is, I'm pretty sure she *did* tell me she was coming by. Maybe I didn't want to believe it. Maybe I made myself forget, even though she's been around the house a few times since she finished up her freshman year at the University of California at San Diego. She stopped by with

18

Kate a week ago and brought me that homemade lasagna that she'd cooked herself, since Holland has a magic touch with pasta. "You didn't think I was going to let you get ready for graduation all by yourself, did you?"

"Pretty sure I can get ready by myself."

"Well, it's not like I brought makeup or five different outfits for you to choose from," she says, and lets herself in. It's just us alone in my house. I could shut the door and pull the blinds and watch movies on the couch with her all day. We could hole up here and never leave, just Holland and the dog and me. Order Chinese takeout from Captain Wong's around the corner for every meal. Yes, this is how I could get through an endless summer on a lonely planet.

Holland peers down the hall. "Where's you-know-who?"

"Who would that be?"

She waves a hand dismissively. I know she means Trina. I just want her to say it. I want to know she's bothered by the hot doctor who hangs out at my house.

"Dr. Asvati," Holland says, drawing out the name, like it's an insult. Maybe it is to her.

"Trina."

"Trina," Holland repeats, the word heavy in her mouth. She's jealous. She *has* to be jealous. This is excellent. I would like her to be jealous.

"She's not here."

"She's not coming to your graduation?"

I shake my head. Trina and I don't have that kind of relationship.

Holland walks to the living room and sits down next to my dog. She pets Sandy Koufax's ears and talks to my dog in a high-pitched voice, telling her she is the cutest dog in the whole wide world. Sandy Koufax rolls over and lets Holland pet her belly. Seeing the two of them like that, the girl who likes the dog, and the dog who likes the girl, makes me want to blurt out the invitation: *Let's shack up here all summer and not leave until August.* Maybe she'd feel sorry enough for me to say yes, to stay, to say leaving me last fall was the dumbest thing she ever did and *will you please take me back?*

Why yes, Holland, I think I would take you back. Even though I don't have a single clue as to the secret of why you left me in the first place.

Holland points to my cap on the coffee table. "This cap thing. Pretty sure it's supposed to go on your head."

"That's what all the graduation how-to books say."

She grabs the cap and walks back to me. She hands me the mortarboard and I put it on, far back on my head.

"That's all wrong." Holland laughs, shakes her head, as if this is normal, as if she can just slide into the way we used to be good buds before last summer, before everything else. "It's supposed to sit on your forehead." She mimics pulling a mortarboard down on her forehead, pointing to this spot right above her eyes where the cap is supposed to rest.

"Fix it," I say, and it comes out raspy, like a croak. I know I should say *please fix it* or *can you fix it?* but this is all I can manage, this two-word admission, as I do everything not to sound hungry for her.

"See! You did need me to get ready," she says, then looks at me, half-nervous, like she's waiting for an answer, waiting for me to admit I needed her.

I just point to the cap. She nods, then wiggles the cap farther down my forehead. Her fingers brush against my face. My heart pounds a tick louder at her touch, but I look away, because the ache is too much. She pulls my cap down for a final tug, then stops to consider a strand of my brown hair. "I can't believe my mom didn't make you get a haircut for your graduation."

"Yeah, oddly enough she doesn't really control my hair."

"She thinks she controls everything," Holland says, and rolls her eyes like she's trying to invite me back into the teasing, to the way we make light of Kate and her tendencies. I say nothing, and Holland absently taps the silver chain on her neck that she wears every day. There's a small circle hanging from it and the name SARAH is engraved on it. Sarah was Holland's friend from college who died a few months into their freshman year. Then Holland says softly, "You always look so nice when you get your hair cut."

"Do you want me to get a haircut?" I want to kick myself the second the words come out.

"Your hair looks great. So does the rest of your *ensemble*," she says, gesturing to my cap and *robe*. "Mom will approve too." She catches herself. "Sorry. I meant my mom."

"It's okay. I know what you mean."

"Do you miss her today?"

"I miss her every day," I say instantly, relieved that someone has asked, that someone wants to know.

"Of course. That was stupid to ask."

"You can ask. You're the only one who does," I say, because after two months, the condolences are running out, and it's as if my mom is being erased from the world again as the memory of her fades and we all start to forget. But Holland's asking, Holland's remembering, and I want to grab her and tell her, *Everything hurts, and I can't stand the hurting.* Instead my hand lifts a few inches, like it has a mind of its own and wants to touch her, to connect with her through words and skin. But I don't go that far. I can't stand the hurting.

"I miss her too. I miss planting flowers with her, and I miss going to the farmers' market with her, and I miss looking at all those bulb catalogs with her," Holland says, and my heart rises in my throat because *Holland hasn't forgotten either. She hasn't forgotten a thing.* "And now the cymbidium, the boat orchids in front of your house? The ones I planted with her last summer? They need to be trimmed."

"Yeah?"

"She would have done that. She would have trimmed them around now."

I can see it so clearly. I can picture my mom outside the house, wearing jeans and a T-shirt because she was a jeans-and-a-T-shirt kind of mom, planting the orchids last summer, hoping she'd be here a year later to take care of them. Determined to be here a year later.

"Right. She would have," I say quietly, then I steer away from all this, from these cracks in my chest that feel too much like feelings. "I don't see why I have to go to graduation, though. My mom was the one who liked all these ceremonies and crap."

Holland tilts her head to the side. "Do you want to skip it?"

I scoff. "What? Are you serious?"

"I am serious, Danny. If you want to skip graduation, I'll cover for you."

The idea entices me. "What would you say?"

"I don't know. I'll come up with something. I'll pretend I'm you!"

I laugh.

"I mean it, though. If you need to escape or whatever, I'll go out there right now and I'll tell my mom you're on your way, that you want to drive yourself. And we'll go without you. And when they say your name, I'll act like I have no idea where you are. Or I'll get up and say you took the dog for a walk. Do you want me to?"

"You would do that?"

"Yes."

"You would really do that?"

"I would really do that. I would do that for you."

She is serious. She will do this for me. I hate her for breaking me so many months ago, and I love her for wanting to cover for me today.

But this isn't about Holland, and this isn't about me. "I should go. For my mom."

Holland nods. She knows this is what my mom was holding on for. Kate does too. Kate said it all the other day when I told her I didn't want to go. *Elizabeth loved ceremonies. Elizabeth loved events. This was the thing she was trying to live for. For the last five years, all she wanted was to make it to your graduation before she died. So get up there and give your valedictory speech so your mother, wherever she is, can hear you.*

Kate doesn't believe in heaven or the afterlife. My mom didn't either. We're Jews, and Jews don't subscribe to the typical heaven or hell ideas. Kate does believe my mom is somewhere, maybe in limbo, maybe in spirit, waiting for this moment. Why, then, didn't she hang on? I wish there were an answer, because I just don't get why my mom could survive five years of remission and recurrence and come up eight weeks shy of the thing she held on for. But there's no one here to ask. When my dad died, my mom was there to answer the unanswerable, to make sense of the fault line in our life—and we got through that somehow; we came out on the other side. Now I'm 0 for 2 and I don't get any more pitches to swing at.

And so it must be time for my friend Vicodin.

I slip into the kitchen to take a pill, and when I return to the hall, Holland gestures to the front door. "My mom and dad are waiting outside," she says. "We'd better go."

Then I'm piling into the car with them, driving to the

place I'll never have to step foot in after today, and I'm marching with the rest of the class, I'm sitting down listening to the principal, then he's calling me to the stage for the final time. My last assignment; then high school will be behind me and college in front. Just one summer in between.

"Daniel Jon Kellerman, our valedictorian."

I walk to the podium, take out my index cards, and look at my classmates in the first several rows. We all look like otters, just a fat sea of otters, with blond hair or brown hair or red hair, with tanned skin or black skin or white skin. They're not the ones I want to see. There's only one person I want to see in the audience. I even begged my mom at one point to hold on. Begged her like a little kid would do. A couple months ago when it was clear she was nearing the end, I pleaded, "June's not that far away. You can do it, Mom."

What a shit thing to do. What a shit thing to ask.

I worked my ass off through high school. I had my nose in all the books; I was not going to let valedictorian slip from my grasp. She knew I had a good shot, knew I was in contention. *My son, the valedictorian.* I pictured her saying it today, bursting with pride, with joy. It was like this thing I could give her, a last gift to her. But she doesn't even know I pulled it off because I got the news I was top of the class three days after she became ash. And I'm flesh, and I don't want to be here on this stage. I want to lie down on a raft, close my eyes, and let the little white pill take me away, float me off into the happy land where I feel no pain. It's kicking in, and so the words I'm saying, sounds and syllables about this moment, about the future, don't matter to me, and they don't matter to all these people out here in the audience. My words don't change how they see me.

The orphan.

The dad was killed in an accident six years ago.

Then the mom died in April.

Remember the sister? She's gone now; she took off for China years ago. Does anyone even hear from her?

They all think they know me. Because that's all I am to them—that guy with the shitty luck.

I glance down at my index cards and do the thing they most want me to do. Because I can be that guy now. I can be mercurial. I can be fickle. I can be the guy who gets away with anything, and for the first time in months—years—I am grateful I have carte blanche to say whatever I want.

I stop reading. I rip the index cards in half and fling the severed blue remains up in the air.

"Fuck high school. Fuck everyone. I'm outta here."

Let me tell you: You've never seen a standing ovation like that before.

Chapter Four

My mom would have flipped out if she knew what I did. She would have gone ballistic and slapped me upside the head.

Not literally. She never hit me, obviously. But she would have given me all kinds of stern looks and disappointed glares. *I did not raise you to tell your peers to fuck off, Daniel Kellerman.*

She expected a lot of me. When I was in fourth grade working on a book report, she made me start the whole thing over when she read it and said it was barely even legible.

"What's wrong with it?" I asked her.

"It's not good enough yet. You have to try harder," she said, her voice gentle. "You have to try hard at everything you do. That's all I ask."

I rolled my eyes and revised it, and over time her approach wore off on me and I became like her too—wanting to do my best, expecting my best.

That's why I can't face Kate. She knew my mom better than anyone, and Kate probably wants to wallop me right now. Because I did the absolute opposite of what my mom would have expected or wanted. I leave Terra Linda before Kate can find me. I walk home, since it's only a couple miles away, chucking my cap and robe into a trash can on a street corner, then I change into gym shorts when I get home and head to the garage, my dog following close behind as I park myself on the gym bench out here. Yeah, this is my life. Working out on graduation. What could be better than this?

But I don't want to go to a party, and I don't want to have some fancy meal at some fancy restaurant with people who are pissed at me, or people who feel sorry for me, or people who feel both, not to mention my own disgust at what the guy on the stage wearing my cap and *gown* just did.

Besides, I have to figure out what to do with all our *stuff.* Kate may be the executor of my mom's will, but Laini and I are the ones she's executing for, and there's so much *stuff* to figure out, money to be moved around, accounts to be administered, possessions to be dispersed.

Like wigs. Like, what do I do with all those wigs?

I manage a dry laugh, because it was so much easier—*easy* being an incredibly relative term—when my dad died. My mom handled it all. She managed all the phone calls and decisions while Holland made brownies and showed me stupid cat videos on the Web to try to make me laugh again. Because that's what my dad and I had always done together—*fun*. We did *fun* incredibly well. We'd spend entire Saturdays in the pool, inventing games and racing each other. We'd go out for doughnuts or ice cream and talk about random things. We'd read every book in the Get Fuzzy collection together. When he was gone, that fun rudder was out of whack, and Holland was determined to fill the role of humor producer in my life. She did it ably, all while my mom kept us going as a family.

But now my parental insurance policy has run all the way out, and so it's up to my sister and me to figure out things like wigs and college funds and the apartment in Tokyo.

I start chest presses and let my thoughts turn to Tokyo, where I was born, since my parents both worked for Japanese companies at the time. We moved back to California when I was three, but we kept returning to Tokyo for vacations. Now we have a place there, an apartment in the Shibuya district, the center of young Tokyo, with neon and lights and billboards the size of Mars, with shops and stores open at all hours and über-trendy girls who *click-clack* down the sidewalks in gold high heels and playing-card earrings, and dudes who wear plaid pants and black lace-up boots.

Back when we were a foursome, we'd spend summer breaks and winter breaks in Tokyo. My dad, my mom, Laini, and me. Eating noodles and fish, buying manga I couldn't read, asking whoever walked past to take our picture.

I haven't been to Tokyo in a year because I was too busy as a senior—too many tests, assignments, college apps, and so on. But my mom traveled there to see Dr. Takahashi, who runs a clinic for cancer patients that's part Eastern medicine, part Western medicine. For her first trip to see him, I drove her to the airport and walked her to security. She was practically bouncing the whole way. "If there is a miracle cure, this is it. *He* is it," she said. She believed in him, and so I did too, especially when she felt better than she had in years. It was working, his mix of traditional medicine and alternative treatment. Takahashi was my mom's last great hope, so she saw him at least once a month in the last year. Filled with hope each time. I was filled with hope each time. For a while there, all that hoping brought its rewards.

Now all I have is an apartment in Tokyo to show for so much wishing, so much wanting.

Because Laini told Kate last week—*e-mailed* Kate, I should say—that it was entirely up to me to decide what to do with the apartment in Shibuya.

Do I keep it or sell it? Rent it? Or say to hell with California and set up a new home far, far away from here?

I risk a grin at the thought. Because there's a part of me that likes that idea. Get out of town and never look back.

I switch to the dumbbells, working on triceps, then biceps, thinking of the empty apartment, picturing dust gathering on the wooden slats of the futon in the room I slept in. I've never had a bad time in Tokyo. Never had a bad time at all.

Maybe it's time for me to go back.

I put the weights away and turn to Sandy Koufax. "Do you want to go for a walk?"

She wags her tail. She likes the word *walk*.

I go back into the house, ignoring the texts from Kate and Jeremy and Ethan and everyone else. I close the piano, duct-tape it shut in several places, and then slap a sign on it that says DON'T TOUCH. REALLY. DON'T TOUCH.

I leave the door unlocked so Jeremy and Ethan can come by whenever they want and do whatever they want. It's an arrangement that works; I barely have to say a word, but there are people around now and then, making the house a little less empty. Then I leash up Sandy Koufax to take her for a hike in the Hollywood Hills. As we cover the hard-packed trails, I tell her about my last trip to Tokyo a year ago. I tell her about visiting the fish market while my mom wore her pink wig, about eating some strange octopus pan-cake from a street cart near the University of Tokyo, and I tell her about the time I wound up having lunch with a group of Japanese college students who invited me to join them at their table while they were playing a party game with chopsticks that made no sense to me, but everyone was laughing, and soon I was too. Maybe I could find them again. Go back to the same restaurant, learn how to play that chopsticks game.

I tell her all this and more, and soon we've traversed miles, and the sun is so low in the sky that the paths are all shadow now. I find my way back to the rental car Kate got for me and open the front door for Sandy Koufax. She hops up on the passenger seat and curls into a ball, panting. I blast the AC for her as I drive.

I park several houses away because there are cars everywhere, jammed up against every square inch of sidewalk, and the noise and the music and the madness is spilling out from my house and my yard and my pool. I'm surprised the neighbors aren't complaining, but I guess I still have that free pass, so no one is saying anything as all of Terra Linda celebrates in my house.

Have pool. Have fridge. Have at it.

I steal inside, a quiet thief, and no one notices the host, the man of the hour—and that's fine because I like noise much more than I like quiet.

Besides, there's a part of me that's already out of the country anyway.

Chapter Five

I clean up the next morning, dragging a garbage bag around my yard, tossing away the remnants of the party that became the background to another night in this house. Everyone is gone now, but I haven't told anyone that I'm thinking of getting away. That I'm thinking a quick trip might be just what the doctor ordered. Besides, I've got to treat the Tokyo apartment like an investment, and to do that I should evaluate it closely, inspect it, consider it.

Right?

It would take my mind off this looming summer that stands like a cavern between today and the start of college, when I can bury myself in classes and get away from my house and all its rooms that echo, all the rooms I don't enter anymore. Or maybe I should just spend the summer volunteering. Go to the library, shelve books, listen to that old, grizzled surfer dude who spends his days checking books in and out, chatting with patrons. I could smile and nod as he tells me about the waves he used to catch in the Pacific. I wouldn't have to say a word. I'd just be his audience, and it'd be air-conditioned.

It's not as if I can play baseball like I used to in the summers. My baseball-throwing arm, which for years lobbed hardball after hardball, is shot, courtesy of a shoulder injury junior year. And it's not as if I'm going to be taking care of my mom or going to the movies with Holland. It's not as if I have any plans at all for the next three months.

I grab the last bit of party debris and head back inside. As I toss the bag, my phone rings. Holland's picture appears, and some vestige of self-preservation tells me to bury the phone in the couch cushions. But my desire for her is stronger, and it wins.

"Hey," she says, speaking first.

"Hey."

"Remember that guy who used to paint himself in silver and do all those robot moves on the Promenade?"

"Sure."

"And how he never talks? Even if you talk to him, he stays in full robot mode?"

"Right."

"Well, he just got in a fight with some other robot. A gold robot!"

I laugh. "Like, did they hit each other?"

"They were about to, then some cop broke it up. Apparently the gold one was horning in on the silver one's turf."

"Crazy," I say, picturing painted-robot-people fisticuffs. That would have been a good way to kill an afternoon.

"So," Holland starts, and then stops, as if the words she was about to say have vaporized. She finds them somehow. "So I was going to get lunch. Do you want to join me?"

"Yes," I say, and within seconds I'm in the car and on my way to her.

I find her at an outdoor café. She's wearing big brown sunglasses pushed up on her head. The sun is bright, but she's not shielding her eyes. She's looking right at me as I walk toward her and sit down next to her. She's got on a short skirt, this green corduroy skirt that she wore when we went to the movies one time last summer and sat in the back row and barely watched a scene on the screen.

I can smell lemon-sugar lotion on her too. Her lotion, her scent.

"I love this weather," she says, and tilts her face to the sun. She closes her eyes and soaks in the rays, and I have free rein to look at her. At her neck, her throat, her shoulders, since she's only wearing a tank top. Forget the library volunteering. Maybe Holland will take me to lunch every day this summer. Maybe she'll sunbathe, and I'll pass the days watching her.

She opens her eyes, sees me looking at her. But she doesn't look away, nor do I.

"Because, you know, I'm allergic to cold."

"And fog," I add, because I know this riff, I know how she feels about hot and cold, and it is so easy to slide back into our banter, our back-and-forth.

"And any temperature below seventy degrees."

"And windchill."

"*Windchill.* The worst thing ever invented."

"And snow. And ice."

"Of course. Let's not forget ice," she says, and mock shudders. Then the waiter comes by and asks what we want.

She orders a sandwich, and I do the same. Same orders, same choices, same food we used to pick when we came here before. A group of friends about our age sits down at the table next to us. Two girls, two guys. One of the girls has short blond hair, the other a blue streak in her hair, and they're laughing about no more boarding school and talking about the start of Juilliard, it sounds like.

"So about graduation," Holland begins.

I hold up a hand, reflexes kicking in. "Is that why you asked me to lunch? Because I really don't want to talk about it. I'm sure your mom already reamed me out on my voice mail."

"You think that's what I'm going to do?"

Like I have *any* idea what she's going to do anymore. Like I had any clue she was going to excise me from her life after all her promises, all her words, all the ways she told me we weren't like any other high school couple, that we were different, that we could last. She repeated all those promises, and so did I, the day she drove off to San Diego. I believed all of them. Every single last one. And then, poof. She pulled her disappearing act.

And yet, here she is, inches from me, her bare legs close enough I could run a hand over her knee, watch her shiver and smile, and then she'd ask me to do it again. My body is filled with complete emptiness and complete longing at the same time, only there's not enough space in me for both, so they fight and argue and run masking tape down my middle to divide me.

"I thought it was awesome. Like, the kind of epic thing people will be talking about for years. *Remember the time Danny Kellerman told us all to eff off?*"

"I believe the words were *fuck everyone*, Holland." I cannot resist teasing her on this front. She has never sworn. She has never lobbed the F-bomb.

"Bleep," she says. "Besides, you didn't miss much. I mean, you were at my graduation dinner. It's just a chance for people to tell embarrassing stories about you."

"Like the time you threw your copy of William Faulkner's *As I Lay Dying* into the pool, calling it *As I Lay Failing*?" I say, recounting the stories that were shared one year ago when Holland finished high school and my mom and I joined her family for dinner.

"That is the cruelest novel ever assigned to high school seniors."

"Or how you'd announce every few months that you had a new plan for what you wanted to study in college. Some days it was environmental science; some days it was French

37

history," I say, prompting another trip back in time, and I don't know why I'm doing this, why I'm acting as if we're still those same people who went to dinner together with our families a year ago. Except that it feels good to remember when I was happy.

Holland and I were together the summer before my senior year at Terra Linda and her freshman year at UCSD. It all started after I gave her that star ring. I was crazy nervous to give it to her because even though I *knew* something had been brewing between us, with every innuendo and flirtation, I didn't entirely *want* to let myself believe it. I fooled myself into thinking I was just giving her this silly ring, a cheap little decoder ring, like the kind of thing you'd find in a gumball machine. I went over to her house, and both her parents were out, and it was the middle of the day, so Holland was doing what any self-respecting California girl who'd just graduated from high school would be doing. Hanging out with all of her friends by the pool. Caitlin and Anaka, Elle and Lila. I was outnumbered, and clearly there were too many bikinis and too much flesh for me to be able to see straight, or be able to give a girl a gift and not feel supremely stupid.

But Holland didn't care that her friends were over. Her face lit up when she answered the door. "Come join us, Danny," she said, and waved toward the pool.

"I have to be someplace," I said, and thrust the box with the ring at her.

"Come on. Stay. Please stay."

"I have to go."

Later that night, she found me on the beach as I walked Sandy Koufax on the edge of the waves. She marched up to me and held up her hand. The ring was on her right index finger. "I *love* this ring, Danny. I love this ring so much."

My heart ricocheted around my chest. "You do?"

"I do."

A step closer. It was like a slow dance, and you know what's coming next, you know you're coming together, and it's all a delirious build.

"Do you remember that time you helped me with calculus earlier this year?" she began.

"Yes."

"And how you didn't make fun of me for not getting integers or derivatives or whatever it was?"

"Why would I have made fun of you for that?"

"Because you're smarter than me."

"That's not true," I said. I was just good at school.

"But the point is, I wasn't embarrassed to ask you and I knew you'd help and you did help. Or how about all the times you drove me to school and you always came to the door to get me? You never honked."

"My dad always told me to never honk when you pull up to someone's house. Turn off the car and walk to the door to get them."

"Or how about the time my mom and dad were out of town and I found a possum in the house?"

"He was pretty creepy." I laughed, remembering the possum under the couch.

"And the first thing I did was call you. And you came over right away."

"Well, you *did* shriek a bit on the phone. But yeah, you had a possum under the couch. Of course I would come over," I said, and I felt like every breath was magic in the night air, because I knew every breath would bring me closer to her. "But it wasn't me who saved you from the possum." I tipped my forehead toward my dog. I had brought Sandy Koufax over, and she ferried that possum right out of the house and into the backyard. Holland slammed the doors shut, then insisted on cooking a steak for my dog, who stood at the sliding-glass doors looking out all night and watching for the possum she'd almost had for dinner.

"The point of all this is—you're awesome. So it's about time we just admitted it."

I inched closer to her. This was happening. This was real. "Admitted what?" I asked, teasing her.

"This." Then her arms were around my neck, and my lips were on hers, soft and warm and better than in all the times I'd imagined kissing her. Her perfect body was pressed against mine, and my mind was soaring, and my whole body was humming.

At the end of the summer Holland went off to college, but we had plans. We were going to see each other twice a month. I'd drive down there, or she'd drive up here every other weekend. But the first time I was supposed to visit, my mom needed a blood transfusion, and even though Kate kept saying she'd take care of her that weekend, I wasn't going to leave my mom alone. I canceled, and we made plans for two weeks later. But then Holland called and told me she had a massive project due in her women's studies elective that Monday morning and if I came down she wouldn't touch the thing, she'd only touch me, and so she had to resist me, a sentiment that was ridiculously endearing at the time.

The next time we talked, she was a different person entirely. It was as if a machine inhabited her and moved her mouth with its robot hands and turned her voice into a cold talking computer. "Danny, I'm in college now. I need to get my head on straight. I need to focus."

A clean break.

I didn't see her again until my mom's memorial service. She even read at the service, a line from *The Little Prince*, something about living in the stars, or laughing in the stars, or something that basically is supposed to comfort you and shred your heart at the same time. I near about lost it when she got up and read, and she pretty much did too.

Now we're having lunch.

"Well, college sucks," Holland says after the waiter brings her an iced tea. "I hated literally everything about my freshman year."

"You did?" This is news to me. Then again, everything about her life for the last several months is news to me.

"Every. Single. Thing."

She reaches a hand to her throat, feeling for her necklace, touching the tab with the word SARAH on it. I watch her fidget with it before she lets it go to take a drink. Then I realize why she'd say college sucks. Her friend died.

Soon we're eating our sandwiches, and she's paying the bill, even though I try many times, but she keeps insisting. I thank her as we walk away from the café. She stops, takes a deep breath, and turns to me. "Do you want to go to the movies?"

"The movies?"

"Yeah, that thing where they project two hours of famous actors in impossible situations on the screen?"

"I'm familiar with the concept."

But *movies*? That was what we did *before*. We watched big shoot-'em-up action flicks. "The more stuff that blows up, the better," was Holland's mantra. She had no interest in Oscar contenders, or quiet dramas, or period romances with English accents. "I want fires, and I want chase scenes, and I want dudes jumping out of tenth-story windows and then running through the streets like it didn't even hurt."

I wanted the same. Life was full of enough family drama. I didn't need it on the screen.

"There's a new Jason Statham flick at the theater down the block, I hear," she says, throwing out the name of our favorite action star. "We could get popcorn and gummy bears."

That was where we saw movies last summer, when we were together.

"What do you mean?" I ask as my heart pounds against my skin, trying to make a mutinous escape to land in her hands. Does she mean go to the movies like we did when we were friends, or when we were *more*? Because she alone could give me my reason to stay in California, if she wanted *more*.

"Want to go? You know, for old times' sake."

Right. For old times' sake. Because we should be buds again, not more.

"I'm not really up for a movie." Movies, lunch, graduation-morning pop-ins—I don't need her pity. I don't need her trying to resurrect our friendship because she feels sorry for me.

"Do you want to take Sandy Koufax for a walk then? We could walk and talk."

"Talk?" That four-letter word sounds so alien, like she's speaking another tongue now.

"Sure. *Talk*," she repeats, all tentative, like she's not even sure how she's forming words either.

"I've got plans with Trina," I say as I walk away so she can't see my face as I lie to her.

"Danny."

I turn around, and she looks like a snapshot, like she's been caught taking one step toward me.

"What?"

"Nothing," she says quickly. "It's just…I trimmed the boat orchids earlier today. They look better now."

43

Chapter Six

The next day I check the mail for the first time in a week. There are no more sympathy cards. They have all come and gone. The *sorry*s, the prayers, the *my thoughts are with you*s are over. Everyone has said what they need to say to the bereaved, and everyone has moved on to their happy, joyful, noisy, everyday lives.

The mail brings only memories. Catalogs from gardening-tool makers. Order forms from bulb suppliers for tulips, calla lilies, dahlias. There is even some flyer from this environmentally friendly tree company offering my mom a lilac bush. She loved lilacs. They were her favorite. Wild lilacs on trees. She stopped and smelled every lilac bush she ever saw, I'm sure. Every now and then she'd cut off a branch and put it in a vase, but lilacs were best enjoyed in the wild, she said. Then she'd wink and add, *The wilds of Los Angeles*.

For Mother's Day when I was ten, I woke up early and left the house with a pair of garden clippers. We had a neighbor a few blocks down who had a huge lilac bush on the side of his house. He was one of those dudes who didn't like kids, though, one of those *get out of my yard, you whippersnapper* types. But my mom coveted his lilacs. So I sneaked into his yard, snipped off a few branches, and ran back down the street to our house. I placed the lilacs in a glass and handed them to my mom when she woke up.

"You little scofflaw," she said when I told her the story.

"Do you like them?"

"Love them. They're perfect."

The next few days she sniffed them every chance she had.

I drop the catalogs and everything else from the mailbox into the green recycling bin at the end of the driveway. As the papers fall, I see Mrs. Callahan from across the street. She's in her porch swing, drinking a glass of iced tea. She holds a book in her hand and waves to me. "Good afternoon, Daniel," she shouts.

I wave back and turn around to head inside. I glance once more at the green bin, and just by chance—by sheer, dumb, accidental luck—I see something that doesn't look like a catalog. It's a letter, a handwritten one, practically an ancient artifact these days.

I reach for the envelope. It's addressed to me, my name written like it's calligraphy in some sort of felt-tip pen. The

postmark is Japanese and the name in the return address—
Kana Miyoshi—is so familiar. My brain is feeling pin-
pricks, like someone is tapping needles against my head,
trying to drum up a memory. *Kana Miyoshi*. I say the name
silently, then whisper it. "Kana."

My mom mentioned Kana a few times. Kana is the teenage daughter of the woman who took care of the apartment
when my mom wasn't there. Kana lives in Tokyo. Kana
knew my mom.

Kana knew my mom.

Everyone else is forgetting my mom. But maybe this girl
remembers her.

I peer quickly at Mrs. Callahan. She is watching me
without watching me, her eyes alternating between her
book and me. I know she doesn't have bionic eyes. I know
she can't read the letter from across the street.

Still, this is not a letter I will open in front of anyone.

I walk back into my eerily quiet house and sit down at
the kitchen counter. I slide a thumb under the envelope flap,
but before I rip it open I realize my hand is shaking. My
heart is beating quickly too, like I expect this letter to
unleash secrets. I know it's not from my mom; I know that.
But right now it's the closest I'm going to come to a connection to her. To anyone.

I turn to my dog.

"It's a letter from Kana," I say to Sandy Koufax, who's
stretched out on the nearby couch. Her legs poke up in the

air. The back ones look like drumsticks with those meaty thighs she has. She tilts her head toward me. "What do you think it says, Sandy Koufax?"

Sandy Koufax listens to my question and waits for an answer.

I pull out the letter and I feel like I'm not in Los Angeles anymore. I'm thousands of miles away, in Japan, in Tokyo, in the Shibuya district. I try to shake it off, but as I unfold the letter, I can see and smell and hear and taste Tokyo. Even the paper looks Asian.

Dear Daniel—

Greetings! I am Kana Miyoshi and my mother, Mai, is the caretaker for your apartment on Maruyamacho Street. We were cleaning the apartment recently and we discovered several medication prescriptions on the shelves.

She lists the medicines and notes whether each bottle had been opened. Most are marked as unopened. Odd.

Would you like us to ship them to you, leave them here, or dispose of them? I am sorry to trouble you with this seemingly trivial matter, but we must be careful with how we handle medication and other related items.

Please advise.

Also, it is customary in situations like this for us to inform the family of the personal effects in the apartment.

Then she lists things like clothes and photos and other items, but what catches my attention are the next few lines.

I have sorted through the bills, and I have gathered the cards and the letters. I can send them along if you wish, or leave them here.

There are also several crossword-puzzle books, a packet of lilac seeds, and your mother's pink wig. Perhaps you know it? It is the hot-pink wig, and, as I'm sure you know, it was her favorite. She must have left it here on her last visit in the winter. She wore it when we visited her favorite temple. I have a photo from that day, which I can send, along with any other items you might want.

Your mother was a lovely woman. We had tea with her occasionally at the Tatsuma Teahouse, where she told us such beautiful stories of her family, especially you. She was quite fond of the teahouse and liked to laugh and say that she was just following doctor's orders by going there. I would also like to let you know that she was always happy when she was here. She was the

most joyful person I think I have ever known,
perhaps especially in the last few months.

Best,
Kana

Then there's a phone number and an e-mail address under her name. But I don't dial and I don't type because I'm already up the stairs, turning the corner, opening the door to my mom's room for the first time in two months, a room I've avoided purposefully because the emptiness might kill me. I don't look around; I head straight for her bathroom.

I yank open the medicine cabinet, hunting for pill bottles. But there are none in here. Just toothpaste, lipstick, nail polish, lotion, and a nail file. Did Kate clean them out? Dump out the unused meds? She's the only other person who's been in the house. I close the mirrored door quickly and open the drawers below the sink to find towels, tissues, and a hair dryer that was hardly used in the last few years.

I leave, putting blinders on as I pass the bed that's been made for two months, and head back downstairs.

I read the letter again, keying in on the temple and the teahouse this time. My mom e-mailed me every day when she was there for her treatments and talked to me about how good she felt when she came back, but she never mentioned a temple, and she definitely never said a word about Tatsuma anything, certainly not whether the good doctor had sent her to a teahouse, of all places.

49

Each time she returned from a visit, she'd tell me about the treatments, about how the combo of herbs and diet, drugs and medicine, seemed to be working better than anything had before. One time, as we walked the dog to our favorite coffee shop—green tea for her, coffee for me—she said she could *tell*, really tell, as she tapped her heart, as her eyes sparked with hope, that Takahashi's approach was doing the trick.

She was getting well for real, for good.

But then the cancer came roaring back, and when I'd ask her about her visits, about the miracle cure that didn't last, she'd turn the conversation to school, or the dog, or my college plans.

Maybe there was something she wanted to tell me about her time in Tokyo, about her treatments there, about her last great hope, but she couldn't figure out how to say it?

I'm not religious, I'm not spiritual, I don't even know if I believe in anything, yet here is this letter arriving just days after I've started thinking about a trip to Tokyo, and it feels like a message from *out there*.

Because if there are stories about her life that have yet to be told, pieces of her that I *could* still get to know, it's almost as if my mom's not completely gone. Maybe she even meant for me to know them *now*, to find these pieces when I need them most? Because, if there's a little bit of my mom still left in this world, then maybe I won't feel so unmoored all the time. Maybe I can feel that thing called happiness again.

Yes.

This is what I'm supposed to be doing this summer. *This* is how I'm supposed to be passing my days. Figuring out the secret to how she was *the most joyful person* when she was dying. Because I'm living, and I sure as hell don't have a clue how to feel anything but empty.

I flip open my laptop and plug *Tatsuma Teahouse* into the browser, but I can't find a website for it, only a location in Shibuya on a few city guides. There's a short review on one of the sites, so I copy the Japanese words into an online translator, and read the results.

Tatsuma Tea is very healing cure.

The last word tastes like déjà vu.

My mom never talked about this teahouse, but she sure as hell used words like *cure*. I want to smack myself for not having gone to Tokyo with her on her last quest for a cure, for not getting to know the final doctor who took care of her. Because I *get* that green tea is supposed to be good for you and all, but *doctor's orders*? What's that all about?

I could call or e-mail Kana, but I don't want to say the wrong thing to her, to this girl who may hold the key to all the things I don't know about my mom, all the things that would bring a bit of her alive again. Instead I want to take a crazy leap of faith. To go out on the creakiest of limbs and tell the only other person who's not forgetting my mom about this note.

I want to tell Holland. I want to show her the note and study the note and talk about the note and come up with a

51

plan together, a map of what's next. My decision to go to Tokyo is the first thing that's felt like a spark, like a flash of light and color, in months. Because it's *something*; it's movement; it's not just the vast expanse of endless, hollow days.

I grab my phone, keys, and wallet. But when I shut the door, I remember the whiplash of yesterday's lunch. The way we talk to each other like we used to, then the way we don't know how to talk to each other at all. I can't share this letter with someone who knows all of me but doesn't want all of me.

I hop into the rental car and head to the hospital to meet Trina. She's got a break in a few minutes.

In the cafeteria Trina shakes three sugar packets crisply between her thumb and forefinger. She never uses artificial sweetener. "Too many chemicals. That stuff will mess you up," she likes to say. "At least with sugar, we know what it does to you." Then she'll pause and blow air into her cheeks. "Makes you fat!"

She rips open her sugar trifecta and dumps it into her coffee. "Fuel," she says, tapping the paper cup. She wears blue scrubs, a white lab coat, and has her long black hair looped back into a ponytail at the nape of her neck. "So what's the story, morning glory?"

"This chick from Tokyo wrote to me," I say, and tell Trina about the letter as clinically as I possibly can, like an unbiased reporter, because I want her unbiased report in return. Then I tell her about the absence of meds at my house.

"You're going to go, right?"

I don't answer right away, because I expected more back-and-forth. I expected I'd have to convince her. But Trina is decisive, and she has issued a ruling. She leans forward and has this strangely serious look in her hazel eyes, like she's telling the nurse to get the patient into the operating room, stat. "You're going to go over there and meet this girl and read the cards and see this temple and go to this teahouse?"

She chugs half her coffee. I wonder if it burns her throat.

"You *really* think I should go there?" I figured I was crazy. I figured I was casting about for something, anything, and Trina would be the one to knock sense into me. But logical, rational, sensible Trina thinks Tokyo is a good idea.

She nods several times. "Next flight. Go."

"Why?"

"First off, because of the meds. That's a little weird if she wasn't taking them when she was in Tokyo."

"Seriously?"

"Unless she just had them filled. Which could be the case. But yeah, cancer patients usually take their meds. Because, you know, meds make you feel better."

"So I should go to Tokyo, find Takahashi, and ask if my mom was taking her medicine or not?" I ask, sounding like the parent checking up on the sick kid.

"I would, but maybe it's just the doctor in me that's curious about the meds."

"Would he tell me? *Can* he tell me?"

"Sure, I have to imagine he'd talk to you."

"What about the whole doctor-patient confidentiality thing? I thought it was against the rules or something."

She shrugs. "Technically. But that's all about getting sued, and this isn't a TV crime drama. There isn't a trial going on where someone's being compelled to testify." Then she raises an eyebrow and gives me a conspiratorial look. "Look, *I'd* talk to you if I were him, but then again, it's not like I'm an advocate of following all the rules." Trina, of course, has already been a rule breaker. "It's different in Japan too. Doctors there, they're used to talking to the family. Sometimes the family learns stuff before the patient does." She reaches a hand out and places it on mine. "Besides, Danny, what else are you going to do this summer?"

Trina says it so gently, so sweetly, and it's so clear that being with her was never an option for summer entertainment for either one of us. I picture a trip. I could do more than just figure out whether to keep the apartment. I could see the Tatsuma Teahouse for myself, not just read some cryptic online review that hints at a wing-and-prayer kind of hope. I could visit my mom's favorite temple too. I could find the people who knew her, the guy who served her breakfast at the fish market when she was there. I could even meet Dr. Takahashi. I could talk to the doctor—her last great hope—about my mom, about the treatments, find out why she was so damn happy, find out why she couldn't last two more months. I have to imagine he'd talk to me too.

I could learn all her secrets, as if she were still here to tell them to me.

As if she were here to tell me how to be whole again.

"What does she mean about disposing of the meds?" I ask, keeping things practical, businesslike, with Trina.

Trina shrugs. "It's probably the same as here. There's a greater concern in general, at least in this country, about how many meds are now in the water supply. So the government has guidelines for medication disposal. 'Cause otherwise people will dump their unused scrips in the toilet, and then trace amount of drugs get into the water supply," she says, and takes a long drink of her coffee. She sets it down and then slaps her palms against the table, in a sort of punch-line *bah-bump* sound. "That's why I say, *Always finish your PKs, boys and girls.*"

"You know I follow those doctor's orders," I say, then tap the letter. "But what do you think this is all about? This temple and teahouse? Is that like some new medical treatment for cancer? Some alternative healing or whatever?" I don't mention what I saw on that site. It's just a site, just a random comment about tea being a cure. But maybe that's why my mom stopped talking about her visits. Maybe she wasn't just laughing about doctor's orders to go to a teahouse; maybe she really was making a last bet on something iffy and unproven when all the other stuff stopped working. It makes me a little bit crazy that she was grasping at straws, but it's also exactly what I'd do too—fight like hell to hang on, however I had to, by any means possible.

Trina doesn't answer right away. She takes another drink, considering. "I don't know, Danny. I'm a little bit more of a meds gal myself. But whatever it was, it sounds like a good thing, like a good way to go." Her voice softens, like she's talking to a worried patient. "Drinking tea. Sharing stories. That sounds nice, doesn't it?"

I nod briefly and look away. It does sound nice. It does sound pleasant. I'm glad my mom was joyful. I'm glad she wasn't in pain every single second. I hate that she was even in pain at all. Watching her throw up, watching her wither away after treatments—nothing prepares you for that. Not even losing my dad. Because when he died it happened so fast, like a slash. With her, it was a relentless witnessing. And so the days, the weeks, when she felt good were the best. A tear forms somewhere behind my eyes, and I brace myself. I won't cry in front of Dr. Trina Asvati. I won't cry here in this hospital where I met Trina six months ago when she was working on her oncology rotation. I was here every day, and Trina was here every day, and soon Trina and I were making out in supply closets and empty rooms and it was like one of those hospital shows where the doctors and nurses are getting it on all the time. Only, I was the patient's family, but I was eighteen, and Trina didn't care, and I didn't care, and we just fit. Two people who barely had the time or energy or inclination to let another person in. We were perfect for each other.

"Hey," she says softly.

"I'm cool. Don't worry."

"I know. And listen, I'm leaving for Seattle in a week. They're transferring me up there for the rest of my residency."

"Really?"

She nods. "Really. Remember I told you a few weeks ago I was up for a transfer?"

I nod, but I don't remember.

"You know how it goes with these programs. They shift you around."

"Right," I say, but I don't have a clue how it goes with medical programs. I don't even know how old Trina is. I don't ask. She doesn't tell. That's how it's been. I suppose I should feel sad again, pummeled again, but I've got a trip to plan. I've got things to learn about the person I loved most in the world.

I'm suddenly a very busy man.

Chapter Seven

In the parking lot, I look up flights on my phone. I check out prices. I plug in dates. I call Kate as I leave the hospital and head onto the roads back to Santa Monica.

She's driving in her car, and I can tell I'm on speakerphone because one of Kate's many rules is two hands on the wheel at all times. She tells me to meet her at her house in twenty minutes, that both her daughter and her husband are out. She doesn't use Holland's name with me, just says *my daughter*, as if that designation demarcates her into two separate people—the Holland who is Kate's daughter and the Holland who was mine.

When Kate answers the door, she is wearing black workout pants and a black workout top. "I just got back from the gym."

"Good workout?"

"The best," she says as I follow her into the kitchen. Everything is the Best for Kate. She has the best day. The best time. Sees the best movies. Reads the best books. I want to be as happy as Kate someday. She's happy about almost everything. Except losing her best friend, but she is steel, and she won't let on about her own sorrow in front of me.

"I just got three new carpets from my Turkish contact this week." She gestures to the far side of the house. "They're in the *den of iniquity*," she jokes, referring to her rug room, because Kate is the type of person who can joke about her job. She is an antique-rug dealer, peddling fancy, exotic, original, and hard-to-find rugs to the superrich in Southern California. It's not the kind of job you'd ever think someone would have, but she has it, and she does quite well for herself too. Her husband is a tax attorney. It's kind of ironic, in a way, that no one I know has anything to do with the film or TV business, but that's all people think Los Angeles is about.

Kate and I fall into our familiar spots in her kitchen. I head straight for the fridge, reaching for a Diet Coke on the side of the door where they're kept. Kate goes through her regular routine too, filling a glass with her cold, filtered water and adding a slice of lemon to the edge of the glass. I swear, if you saw her water routine, you'd never think this woman worked out at Animal House.

I lean against the counter, taking a drink of the soda,

and then I place the can down. "What do you know about Kana Miyoshi?"

"Mai's daughter?"

I nod.

"What do you want to know about her? They take care of your mother's apartment. Now *your* apartment. They took over the building a year ago from the previous company, so I don't think you ever met them."

"How old is she? Kana."

"She's seventeen. She has one year left in high school, I believe. Are you having some online fantasy relationship with her?"

I laugh silently and shake my head. Kate doesn't mince words. I love her directness on all topics but the one verboten subject that we both know to never broach.

"Why are you asking, then?"

I want to show Kate the letter, but what if she just explains all those things away? What if she just rattles off a quick and obvious explanation of the temple and the teahouse, and then this door is slammed shut? I need this door open.

I shrug. "Curious, okay?"

"It's your standard apartment-management business. Most of the places they manage are owned by foreigners or other people who only go to Tokyo a few times a year. Most don't live there year-round. So they need someone on the ground for any issues or problems with the apartments. That's what Mai does. But she felt her English wasn't good enough, so that's why Kana is so involved. Anything else?"

"Did my mom stop taking her meds when she was there?"

"I don't think so. Why would she do that?"

"Did she stop taking her meds *here*?"

Kate shakes her head. "Not that I know of. Why?"

"Well, where are they?"

"There were things I cleaned out after..." She lets her voice go. Finds it again. "But I didn't inventory her meds. I didn't count pills. Besides, there weren't many left when..." Another deserted sentence. Another side effect of death. Words go AWOL. "So I just got rid of what was left."

Maybe the meds in Tokyo were unopened because my mom had just refilled them on her last trip there. And maybe she never took them simply because she never returned to Tokyo. That would make sense. But even so, I'd like to hear it from the doctor. I'd like to know what the *doctor's orders* were.

Kate takes a few steps closer and puts her hand on my arm. "What's going on, Danny? How can I help you? You know Elizabeth asked me to look out for you, but you should also know that she didn't have to. I'd do it anyway. I love you like you're my own son. And I would be here for you whether she asked me to or not."

I dip my hand into the pocket of my shorts, feeling for the letter but keeping it safe. "I'm going to Tokyo."

Kate takes a minute to digest my news, probably debating whether to weigh in or not. She seems to know her role right now isn't to approve or disapprove. "You are?"

61

"Yes." It's real. It's happening.

"Why?"

"Why not?" I counter.

But before she can respond, her cell phone rings, that grating sound of her ringtone, a James Taylor song. "I'm so sorry, Danny. This will take just one second. It's a client who's been having a problem. And I promised I would sort it out today." In one swift, smooth move, she inserts a headset into her ear and says hello. There's a pause, then she says, "The rugs arrived yesterday. They're fabulous. They're the best. They have this interlocking pattern...."

I tune out the rest as she romances a client. I finish my soda and look around the kitchen and peer down the hall. Even though Holland isn't here, I can't help where my eyes go. That's the hall where her room is.

The call ends, and Kate looks at me again. "Are you okay?"

I nod. "Yeah, totally."

"Come with me. I have to go see this client for literally ten seconds. It's not that far and we'll talk in the car. You and I—we like cars, don't we?" She gives me a smile, trying to get me to laugh. "And I've got the big, comfy Audi with the leather seats. And we'll chat about your trip. And I'll tell you about all the plastic sushi I need you to find for my plastic-sushi collection, okay?"

"I'm fine. You go ahead."

"Then please stay here. Will you? Let's have dinner. I'm ordering Chinese. I'll get your favorite. Pepper steak and sizzling rice soup. I'll be back in thirty minutes. I just have to take care of this. But stay here. Watch TV. Play the Xbox, okay?"

"I have to water the yard," I say, though I haven't turned on the hose in ages. We have a sprinkler system. "I'll just come back in thirty minutes."

Then we're both off, but I don't return in thirty minutes, and I don't water the yard. I buy a one-way plane ticket, since I don't know how long I'll be there. I call Dr. Takahashi's office, and I don't understand a word on his voice mail, but I leave a message asking to see him. Then I e-mail Kana Miyoshi, thanking her for her letter and letting her know I'll be arriving at the end of the week, and I would be so very grateful if she could meet me at the apartment to let me in, since I don't have a key.

Chapter Eight

Two hours later, Holland's at my door. She's holding cartons of Chinese food and her black canvas purse on her shoulder. "I don't think the rice is sizzling anymore, but the pepper steak will taste good if you heat it up."

"Thanks," I say.

"Can I come in?"

I nod, and she walks straight to my kitchen and takes out a ceramic bowl, pours the soup in, and pops it into the microwave. She knows my house as well as I know hers. It's scary sometimes, how much we know about each other. She knows what foods I like, what books I read, what movies I'll watch all the way through and which ones I've walked out on.

I sit down at the counter and let her wait on me because

she seems to want to. She places the soup bowl in front of me, then roots around in the utensil drawer for a spoon. She hands one to me. Next she warms up the pepper steak, then divides it onto two plates. She finds forks and napkins and parks herself across from me, sliding a plate of Chinese food to me and keeping the other for herself.

"I know how much you like Captain Wong's," she says, with a smile that reminds me of all the times we ordered from there.

"I do. But that name kills me every time. *Wong*," I say with a drawl. Then a sci-fi voice. "Hello. I am Captain Wong."

"I have come to take over your planet," she adds. I laugh, and she does too, and then her laughter fades. We eat in silence for a minute, then Holland breaks it. "So you're going to Tokyo?"

"Your mom told you?"

"Yes."

"Did your mom send you to get info out of me or something?"

"No. She mentioned it, and now I'm mentioning it. Why? Is there info to get? Are you going with a girl?"

I scoff. "Yeah, right. I was supposed to go with someone, but it didn't work out," I say, my eyes locked on her the whole time.

"Well, I wanted to go, okay?"

"So did I," I say, so low it's a whisper. But she hears me, and she inches her hand across the counter, just a little bit closer, and that hand, I want to grab it and hold on.

"Me too," she says, barely there, barely painting the space between us with all that has been broken.

I glance at our hands, so close all it would take is one of us giving an inch.

"I bought my ticket an hour ago."

"When do you leave?"

"A couple days from now. I found a good deal."

She nods a few times, taps her fingers. I can feel the warmth from her hands. "Cool," she says, and we stay like that. One stretch is all it would take to be back, so I wait. Wait for her to tell me she'll miss me, to ask me to stay, to put her hands on my face and press her lips against mine and kiss me like it's the thing that's been killing her not to do for all these months. That it's *not* cool for me to go. That if I go, *she'll* be the one who's sad.

But she doesn't. We just finish our food, and she washes the plates, and the other ones that were in the sink too, and she tosses out the cartons from Captain Wong's and bags up the garbage, and she's like a nurse. She's here as a nurse. To take care of me. To make sure I eat enough food and clean the house and take my vitamins.

I watch her take my vitals and check my temperature and adjust the tubes, and when she suggests we watch a movie, here on the couch, I just nod because my heart isn't beating fast enough anymore, blood isn't pumping smoothly enough anymore for me to find the will to say *no* like I did last night. Evidently I can buy tickets to fly out of the country, no problem, but I can't even tell Holland to stop being so near to me all the time but not near enough.

Because she is *supposed* to want to go to Tokyo with me now. She is supposed to invite herself, to ask me in that sweet and sexy, that bold and confident voice, to say that I should take her along, that we promised we'd go together, that we even talked about it last summer.

As if I needed reminding. As if I were the one who'd forgotten.

Instead she turns on the TV and finds a film where the hero survives a bridge being blown up. We stay like that through fire and bombs, through fists and blows, through a knife fight in an alley, a foot away from each other, not touching, not moving, not talking, not curled up together, just staring mutely at the screen.

But faking it becomes too much for me, so when the hero clutches the crumbling concrete from the bridge, scrambling for purchase, I stand up and leave the living room, mumbling, "Be right back."

I walk to the bathroom at the end of the hall. I shut the door. I head straight for the window. I slide it open and pop out the screen. I stand on the toilet seat, then climb the rest of the way out of the window and hop into my front yard. I close the window, and I walk and I walk and I walk.

When I return an hour later, my greatest hope is she'll be gone. My most fervent wish is that I will have made my great escape from her, from her hold on me. But instead I find her sound asleep on my couch, Sandy Koufax tucked tightly into a ball at Holland's bare feet.

I kneel down on the tiles where the book she was reading has slipped out of her tired hands. It's a paperback, *The Big Sleep*. I run a thumb across the cover, wondering when Holland developed a penchant for Raymond Chandler. There was a time when she would have told me her favorite parts. When she would have tried to tell me the ending because she just *loved* it so much, she had to share, and I'd have held up a hand and told her to stop. Laughing all the time. Then I'd have read it too, and we'd have walked on the beach and talked about the best parts. We'd have done that tonight with the movie too. Imitated the actors' inflections at their most over-the-top moments, then marveled at the blown-up buildings.

I shut the book we're not sharing. The ending we're not talking about. I place it on the coffee table and walk upstairs, because if I stay near her, I will wake her up, rustle a shoulder, and ask her. Ask her why she left. Ask her why she's here. Ask her what changed for her.

When I get into my bed, I am keenly aware of her in my house, as if the rising and falling of her breathing, the fluttering of her sleeping eyelids, can somehow be seen and heard from a floor above. I imagine her waking up, walking up the stairs, heading down the hall, standing in my doorway, a sliver of moonlight through the window sketching her in the dark. I would speak first, telling her the truth—

that I'm still totally in love with her. That nothing has changed for me when it comes to her.

Everything else is so muted, so fuzzy, so frayed around the edges. This—how I feel for Holland—is the only thing in my life that has remained the same. Everyone I have loved is gone. Except her. Holland is the before and the after, and the way I feel for her is both lethal and beautiful. It is like breathing, like a heartbeat.

She would say the same words back to me, that she feels the same. Then she would say my name, like she's been searching for something, like she's found the thing she's been looking for.

Come find me, come find me, come find me.

♦ ♦ ♦

In the morning, I find her in my kitchen making toast.

"I am the world's deepest sleeper," she announces by way of a greeting. "I did not wake up once all night."

I say nothing, just sit down at the counter on one of the stools.

"I don't think I even realized I fell asleep. I just woke up this morning all disoriented and then I was like, *Oh, I fell asleep on Danny's couch.*"

The toast pops up, and she begins to spread butter on it.

"But thank you. For letting me fall asleep here."

"Right."

She hands me a plate. I look at the toast like it's a foreign substance. I don't eat it.

"Are you hungry?"

"No."

"Oh."

I push the plate back to her.

"Sorry," she says, and looks down at the plate, staring hard at the toast like it holds secrets. Then she fiddles with her star ring, twisting it one way, then the other.

"Why do you wear that still?"

She looks up, surprised that I've had the guts to ask her a real question for once.

"No, really. What's the point, Holland? Just take off the ring."

She shakes her head.

"Seriously. Take it off. You don't need it anymore. Take the star off and throw it out."

She swallows hard and presses her lips together, as if she is holding back both words and tears. But I *can't* care about her anymore. I can't keep pretending that I've forgotten what we had. Because I haven't, but I can't have her the way I want her. And seeing her here and acting like we're all fine hurts too much. I've got to make the hurting stop.

"I don't want to throw it out," she says. "Okay? I just don't. And if you'd just—"

"Why are you here then? You could have left this morning. You didn't need to make me breakfast. I've been making toast since I was eight. I didn't have to start making toast when my mom died, okay?"

"Danny," she says, and the look on her face is soft, and it's sad, and it *has* to be a harbinger of more pity from her.

"Why did you leave me, Holland? After everything, how could you do it? How could you do it and then just keep showing up like nothing ever happened between us? Because I don't want to *just* go to the movies with you and eat takeout in my kitchen, and I don't want to find you on my couch in the morning. Don't you get it? I can't *just* pretend with you."

She looks hard at me, her blue eyes steely around the edges. "I *do* get it. But there are things that you don't get, and if you'd let me—"

But I feel stronger for the first time in weeks, and lashing out at her feels so good, it feels like survival. "I don't want to go back to being best friends with you. But you're like a disease. You're always around, and you're always showing up, and you act like nothing's changed, but everything's changed, and you—you're like a cancer."

The words come out without warning, too quickly for me to stop them, too fast for me to abort.

I watch as her shoulders drop, her eyes lower, the *thing* I just called her fully registering. She speaks in the lowest possible voice, so low it's a barrier to protect herself from me. "I can't believe you really just said that."

Neither can I. But I know if I open my mouth again, any ounce of self-preservation left in me will wither.

I stare at my plate of uneaten, cold toast as she grabs her book and her black shoulder bag and gives Sandy Koufax a quick pat on the way out before pulling the door closed behind her.

There is nothing, nothing but smoke and dust and debris, here for me in California. The only choice I have, the only *chance* I have, is to leave.

Chapter Nine

We adopted Sandy Koufax two years ago, and she's named after the greatest pitcher ever, a lefty like me, and a Jew.

"We should name her Sandy Koufax," my mom said as I drove us home from the shelter while she petted the little border collie–lab puppy sitting in her lap.

I shook my head. "Sandy Koufax is a guy. This dog is a girl."

She narrowed her eyebrows at me and hugged the dog tightly. "Sandy Koufax is not a sexist pig. She doesn't mind being named after a man."

"Dad would have liked this dog," I said.

She nodded. "He always loved animals."

"He would have been glad we got her from the shelter too."

"He liked shelter dogs best of all," she said.

Sandy Koufax was a fitting name for the dog for other reasons too. He wasn't just the greatest pitcher ever, in my view. He also played through pain, pitching with a damaged elbow, throwing heat with injured fingers. He didn't let the pain stop him. The name would be a fitting tribute not just to my baseball idol but to my mom. Somewhere in the back of my mind I knew the dog would outlive my mom by many, many years. But I wanted to believe that my mom—who was kickass at everything she did—would kick cancer's ass too.

Now Sandy Koufax is all mine. She always was mine, truth be told. The first night home she slept in my bed.

I'm going to miss this dog like crazy.

I drive her to Jeremy's house. His mom and dad love dogs. Like crazy love. They have two Chihuahua–mini pinscher mixes, and Sandy Koufax races to the yard and starts rounding up the diminutive dogs.

"You're the only one I trust to take care of my dog," I remind Jeremy.

"Dude. That dog is in good hands."

"That dog catches Frisbees on the beach. Dogs that catch Frisbees on the beach are hard to come by."

Jeremy points to the tiny beasts in his yard. "*Those dogs* are not chick magnets. I bring those dogs to the beach, and the girls want to take me shopping and ask which shoes to buy."

"My dog is a total chick magnet," I say, and pat Jeremy

on the back. "You will score endlessly with her by your side."

"I'm totally taking her to the pier every day. This is going to be like my most epic summer ever."

"Take good care of her."

"I will. But I'm *not* sending you photos of her."

"But e-mail me, okay? Let me know how Sandy Koufax is doing?"

He laughs and shakes his head. "You're embarrassing. You're like a girl when it comes to this dog."

I call Sandy Koufax over, rub her head, pet her ears, and tell her to be good. She tilts her head to the side, like she's listening. Her tongue hangs out of her mouth. I tell her I love her in a voice so low that Jeremy can't hear me say it. Then we leave, and Jeremy drives me to the plane that'll take me 5,400 miles away.

◆ ◆ ◆

I'm not tired when I file off the plane, pass through customs, and purchase a ticket for the train from Narita Airport into the center of Tokyo. I'm not tired either when I sit down on a red upholstered seat for the quick train ride to the city center. All I feel is relief that I'm far away from California.

I look around at the other passengers, mostly Japanese businessmen and -women returning from their meetings with film execs or record execs or rug-dealing execs or whatever on my same flight from Los Angeles. There are smatterings of families too: moms with toddlers, dads telling those same toddlers to sit down. I don't have to know much Japanese to know what the dads are saying. I see some college students a few rows up—they look European, and they have backpacks slung on their knees for the train ride. They must have rolled off a plane from Germany or maybe Sweden, I guess.

I gaze out the window at the lush, green fields we're passing out in the suburbs that soon turn into the squat apartment buildings at the edge of the city that then become the skyscrapers and sleek, steel structures in the middle of Tokyo. The train arrives gently in Shibuya Station, and I exit, tossing my lone backpack on my shoulder. I packed lightly, not wanting to bother with checked baggage. I stuffed everything I might need—laptop, shorts, T-shirts, some books, and a pair of flip-flops—into an oversize camping backpack. The sneakers are on my feet.

The doors open, not with a screech but with a *whoosh*, and the crowds of people do not push or shove. They politely shuffle off. I'm first, though, hitting the ground of Shibuya Station, taking the stairs out of there two at a time, passing through hordes of Tokyoites who are coming and going from work, from early dinners, from anywhere. It is five thirty in the evening on a Thursday night in June, and the station is bustling. I read somewhere that more than two million passengers travel through this station each day.

I push through the final turnstile at the Hachikō exit.

I'm at one of the busiest, craziest intersections in the world, because Shibuya Station sits at the convergence of six streets that all seem to collide at once, to my American eyes. But somehow the Japanese car drivers and bus drivers and cab drivers all know when to stop, when to merge, and when to let the other lanes go. I walk over to something that has become a favorite thing of mine from all my past trips here. Carved into the street-side wall of the subway station is a bright, chunky mosaic of stars, rainbows, and a white husky dog with a perfectly coiled tail. There's a statue of the dog here too, but I like the mosaic best. Everyone in Tokyo knows the story of the dog named Hachikō. He followed his owner, a university professor, to work every morning and waited for his return in the evenings. One day in 1925, his master failed to show. He had died while teaching. But Hachikō was loyal to the end. The dog walked to the subway stop every day, waiting for the same train for the next several years until his own death. A statue was erected, a ceremony is held every year in April, and the dog's taxidermied body resides in Tokyo's National Museum of Nature and Science.

I tap the dog's head once, for good luck.

I head for the intersection and join the sea of people fanning out in all directions. I don't know any of them, I don't understand any words they say, but there's this flicker, a flash of something familiar inside me, the feeling that I'm no longer so alone.

chapter ten

I open the familiar glass-paneled door to the lobby of our apartment building. I expect to see Kana, since she had told me she'd meet me here at 6:00 PM to let me in and give me my keys. Instead Mai greets me with a small bow, and I bow slightly in return.

"Hello, Mrs. Miyoshi."

"Hello, Daniel. Please call me Mai." She extends her hand, and I shake. She is much younger than I thought she would be. Maybe in her mid-thirties. Her long black hair is fastened in a braid. She wears jeans and a short-sleeve blouse. "How was flight?"

"Good. Easy."

"That is good."

"Yes."

"We are glad. Let me show you." She presses the elevator button, and we shoot up six floors. The last time I was here, my mom was feeling good. She wore an electric-blue wig because her hair hadn't all grown back yet. We went to the fish market every morning for breakfast. "We are so Japanese, aren't we?" she said to me, as we sat at the counter of the food stall we both loved, eating raw fish in bowls.

"Totally, Mom," I said, and then gobbled up more of what had become my favorite breakfast food ever.

The elevator door opens, and Mai gestures for me to exit first. But I sweep out a hand for her. My father would roll over in his grave if I went in anywhere—store, building, car—before a lady. He held doors open for everyone all the time.

Mai walks down the hall, turns the key in the door of our—*my*, I need to get used to saying *my*, especially since I'm the one who has to decide what to do with it—apartment. I follow her in and inhale. My lungs feel like they're filling with the equivalent of water from a fresh mountain stream. This place is small; it *is* Tokyo real estate after all, but it *feels* big compared to my house in Los Angeles somehow. I drop my backpack by the door and turn into the kitchen, running my hand across the outside of the fridge, over the bright white sliver of a countertop, then along the panes of the window that look out over the street below. There are potted plants along the window, some with flowers blooming. They are my mother's plants, the *gardens* she made here in Tokyo so she'd have her flowers here too. I touch the soil in a pot with blue irises. The soil is damp. Mai and Kana must water the plants. I like knowing that they take care of my mom's plants. I lean in to smell the flowers, something my mom did every day. They smell like flowers, like they should, but they also smell like her, if that makes sense.

I return to the living room, breathing in the familiar surroundings—the blond hardwood floors, the bookshelves wedged in that hold framed photos of Laini, Sandy Koufax, my dad from years ago, my mom and me, and then the light-green couch that you just sink into and the metal coffee table where I'd put my feet only to get yelled at for putting my feet on the coffee table.

I can tell the table has been polished and cleaned and shined, but I swear I can see it a year ago, the very last time I was here, with newspapers spread open, ceramic mugs half-drained, crossword puzzles completed. A lazy summer afternoon in Tokyo, my mom wearing a purple wig, a pink wig, one time even a yellow one, drinking tea and doing crosswords. "Ah, I should have retired a long time ago. It suits me so," she said.

I head into the second bedroom—my bedroom. It's just the same. A low futon with a white mattress on hardwood slats, a nightstand, and a slim three-drawer bureau are all that fits in here. I brace myself before I enter my mom's room next, unsure whether the ghosts of the bits of her life here will swallow me whole. But for some reason, seeing her Tokyo bed, her Tokyo nightstand, her Tokyo life doesn't hurt. It feels strangely comforting, maybe even calming. Because this place is breathing, living, pulsing in a way my home in California hasn't in months.

Waiting to share all its secrets with me. All its wisdom. All the things I want to know.

I return to the living room where Mai waits for me.

"You said something about medications, Mrs. Miyoshi? I mean, Kana did. Your daughter did."

"Kana is at practice. She help with that," Mai says in her staccato way of speaking. I wish I spoke better Japanese. I wish I could say more than the basics like *arigato*—thank you—because I'd rather not be the Ugly American who expects everyone to speak his language. But I am. Years of visits, dozens of trips, and I am left bereft of useful language.

"Arigato. Domo arigato."

"Do you need anything?"

I shake my head. "I am good. The apartment looks good. Thank you for taking care of it," I say, then press my hands together and bow once more.

"Kana sees you tomorrow. After school, she says. She will find you at three thirty. I leave now."

I walk to the door and hold it open for Mai, thanking her again and again, as my dad taught me. It's funny to see pieces of him, now and then, in me. But it stings too, because that's all there is now—pieces of memories, and they're becoming more hazy every year. The thought hits me hard that sometime soon, maybe not too far from now, my mom will be faded around the edges as well.

I close the door and am about to head to the bathroom to inspect the medicine cabinet, to get to the bottom of the unused pills. But then I notice the entryway table tucked in the corner. There's the packet of lilac seeds Kana mentioned in her note. Then there are letters stacked neatly in two piles, as promised. One pile has been opened—water bills and stuff like that—and marked *Paid* with an orange Post-it note.

In my mother's handwriting.

Such a pedestrian word, such a functional word—*paid*— but it jolts me because it's her handwriting. *Her* handwriting. It's everywhere at our Los Angeles house if I look around, if I root through drawers and desks and inside boxes. But to see it *here* feels like a trail of bread crumbs, a little bit of hope that if I look hard enough I can find all the pieces of her life left behind, even just the way she sorted through bills and papers while she was here in Tokyo.

The other pile is much smaller, marked with someone else's handwriting, and a pink Post-it that says *Personal*. The stack Kana made when she sorted through this place.

I reach for that pile.

There's an open white envelope, no stamp on it or anything, and inside it is a card, a picture of a black-and-white cat on it. I know instantly it's from Laini. She always loved cats. She had a thing for black-and-white ones especially. Tuxedo cats, she liked to say.

"They always look like they have little white gloves on," she'd say, and then hold her arms out in front of her, as if she were admiring white gloves on her hands. She had a cat growing up. His name was CatCat, and I'm not really sure who named him, but my parents got CatCat for her right after they brought Laini home from China. He was a loyal cat. When she was in seventh grade, he followed her to school one day. She called my parents to come get CatCat and even waited with him in the principal's office until my mom showed up. At dinner that night, everyone sang, "Laini had a little cat, little cat, little cat, Laini had a little cat who followed her to school." He went to "kitty heaven" when Laini was fourteen or fifteen, and she cried for days. My dad even had a little cat memorial service in the backyard that we all attended.

I open the card.

Dear Mom:

I am glad you are my mom.

Love, Laini

It reminds me of the kind of card a grade-schooler sends her parents when she's just learning to write. Then I remember—my mom has a card just like this framed back at the house. It doesn't have a cat on it. But it's on a piece of blue construction paper and written in that blocky, big lettering kids use when they learn to write. The words—*I am glad you are my mom*—are exactly the same. Somehow,

Laini is hearkening back to a card she wrote my mom when she was five.

Is this her way of making good for how she treated our mom? For running halfway around the world and then barely coming back after our mom got sick?

I tuck the card inside the open white envelope when I notice it's not alone. There's a sheet of lined paper folded in quarters inside the envelope, the edges serrated roughly as if ripped from a spiral notebook. My dad kept a stash of standard school-size notebooks on his nightstand. He was always tracking ideas for new businesses he wanted to start. When I was eleven, I noticed him sitting by the pool on a Sunday afternoon writing in a green spiral notebook.

"What are you writing, Dad?"

"Ideas."

"For what?"

"For the day when I won't have to work for the man anymore. Because then I'll invent the sky."

"Sky's already been invented, Dad," I said.

He snapped his fingers in an *aw shucks* gesture. "What about the sea?"

"Sea too."

"And trees?"

"Yes."

"Birds?"

"Definitely," I said, and was cracking up. He liked making me laugh, so we went on like that for several more rounds.

"Seriously, Dad. What are you writing?"

"Just some thoughts on a business I may want to start someday."

"What's the business?"

He looked down at his notes. "Eh, it's not really coming together." He tossed the notebook on the lawn chair and cannonballed into the pool. I jumped in next, and the notebook was forgotten.

Here's a page from one of those notebooks with the top corner ripped off. Only, it's not an idea for a business. It's personal, and it's to my mom. I can barely remember *his* handwriting six years later, but I know he called my mom Liz. He was the only one who called her Liz, and sometimes when he whispered to her in the kitchen or the hall as he pulled her in for a kiss, he shortened her name even more. She was L to him then.

L—

I ALREADY MISS YOU. I WILL BE BACK
SOON. LOVE ALWAYS.

I run a finger over the blue ink, as if I can activate a secret message, a hidden explanation, a translation that will give me a date and an answer to the question that trips through my head: Why is *this* sheet of paper with the corner ripped off in *this* small stack of papers? Why is this tuxedo-cat card here? I know why they're marked *Personal*—they're personal notes, obviously. But why were they important enough to be singled out?

I reach for the last thing in the stack. A sheet of crisp lavender stationery folded in half.

> I ordered these online for you, but they are from the Japanese lilac tree. As you know, they take a few years to bloom, but they will produce the most fragrant and aromatic flowers. It's nice, in a way, to think about flowers to be remembered by, isn't it? And that in a few years, these lilacs will delight people with their scent. Maybe you can find a place to plant them in Tokyo?
>
> xoxo
> Holland

Even five thousand miles away, she is here, inside this apartment, with a note and some sort of parting gift for my mom. I can never get away from her. Only now I am tired of it. I am weary. I am worn down and worn out and worn through. I don't have a clue how to solve the puzzle of Holland. And I don't know if I want to right now, not in this threadbare state of mine. I return to the entryway table and grab the seed package. It's unopened, and I take some small measure of victory that Holland's dreams of lilacs blooming in Tokyo as some sort of memorial to my mom never materialized.

I toss the envelope with the lilac seeds onto the coffee table.

But still, *why* did my mom keep these three notes here? Far away from me. Far away from the house in Los Angeles. Because some are old—my dad's note. And some are clearly new—Holland's letter. Were they all sent to the address of this apartment? Or did my mom bring them on her last few trips to have them with her when she was here? I wish these notes came with a code to decipher them.

But that's it for the *Personal* pile. A note from the daughter who deserted the family, a note from the dad who's long gone, and a note from the ex-girlfriend. All these people who didn't live with her for the last several years. All these people who weren't there every day.

But nothing *from* me. Nothing *for* me.

I could tell myself this is a mere Post-it note from Kana, that it's no big deal to be excluded from this pile. But it's not *just* a Post-it note. It's a collection of things that mattered to my mom. That she must have assembled over the years, gathered together near the end.

I head to the bathroom, yawning as I fumble for the light. Jet lag is kicking in quickly, threatening to smother me into sleep. I slide open the medicine cabinet, and it's filled with prescription bottles. Bleary-eyed, I reach for one. It's a cancer drug, and it's barely been touched. Then another kind. This one was marked "open" on Kana's list, but it looks like nearly all are still in the bottle, like my mom hardly took any. I know these drugs by heart, know their side effects and their benefits.

What I don't know is why they're full.

I remind myself that Takahashi can explain this. Takahashi, the last great hope, the supposed miracle doctor—*brilliant and compassionate*, my mom used to say—will tell me. Rules or no rules. He hasn't called back yet, but I'll go to his office tomorrow.

I grab another bottle. It's Percocet, and it was filled by a pharmacy here several months ago. But even in my barely awake state, I can tell that none were taken either.

Ah, but perhaps *this* is what my mom left for me. Perhaps this is the *Personal* for the son. Yes, a gift from beyond, a beautiful parting gift indeed, because these work wonders on the living. It's such a shame to waste a perfectly good numbing agent. I open the cap and free one of these beauties. I put the pill on my tongue and it feels like blasphemy—taking my mom's painkillers when she was in real pain. But then I do it anyway, swallowing it dry.

I return to the living room, picking up the note from my dad, the card from my sister, the letter from Holland. I fold them all up and put them in my wallet to keep with me at all times.

They are foreign words to me now, but soon, *soon*, I'll know how to translate them. I have to. Really, I have to.

Chapter Eleven

Jet lag wins.

The sun has barely risen, but I'm wide awake, ready for this city to unlock secrets. I shower, pull on shorts, a T-shirt, flip-flops, and sunglasses, and jam my wallet and phone into my pocket. It's too early to meet Kana, too early to find the doctor, so I take the subway to the Tsukiji Fish Market, the largest fish market in the world, stretching along several blocks and all the way out to the Tokyo Bay.

I walk along the edge, where I can hear the merchants inside, sloshing around in their knee-high boots in the fishy water that puddles on the concrete floor as they peddle everything from mackerel to eel to shrimp to salmon to octopus to tuna that was just sold at auction a couple hours ago. I reach the block of food stalls on the outskirts of the market, each one no more than a few feet wide. A red awning with Japanese characters falls over a stall selling fish crackers and dried oysters. Another with bamboo walls is flush against the sidewalk and offers up tempura and soba noodles heated in metal pots.

I find that food stall easily. My first stop. My first order of business. Not just breakfast but maybe a bit of information.

I grab a stool, order, and am quickly distracted from my mission by the taste of raw tuna. It feels like ages since I've enjoyed food, since I've tasted something that made me want food for more than just hunger.

My chopsticks dive into the bowl again, scooping up another heaping spoonful of rice and soy sauce and raw fish. A businessman next to me hungrily spears his breakfast fish too. I look behind the counter, hoping to see Mike. He's this young dude, maybe twenty, who worked here last summer when I visited. He was into music, always playing some cool Japanese tunes on low on his little stereo while he served up fish. We'd sometimes trade song recommendations. If he's here, I'm going to ask him about my mom, what she was like in those final days over here. I'll take an anecdote, a sliver of a tale, something, anything, that'll bring her back in some small way.

Mike's not here, though. Instead there is a hunched-over Japanese woman behind the counter, stirring a huge vat of miso soup, and I ask for a bowl of that too. She nods, then ladles out some soup for me.

I don't even know if this place where I'm eating has a

name. My mom would say, *Let's go to that food stall*, and we'd swipe our subway tickets through the turnstiles and catch an early morning train to the fish market for breakfast. "If sushi cured cancer, I'd be in the clear," she joked last summer over a bowl of tuna.

"Don't say that, Mom. Besides, you will be in the clear soon." She'd held cancer at bay for four years by then. She'd withstood countless rounds of chemo and surgeries. She was going to lick it, I was sure. No one was tougher than my mom. She'd managed the disease with laughter, and some tears, but mostly laughter.

"And then I will be at your graduation, and I will be wearing a neon wig then, not because I need it, but to embarrass you," she teased.

"It would be totally embarrassing," I said, but it also wouldn't be. Everyone at school knew about my mom and her colorful wigs. The girls loved them. They would come up to me, tears in their eyes, and tell me how tough my mom was and how cool she was with her electric-blue wig, her candy-pink hair, her emerald-green curls, and so on.

"You should know I plan on hollering your name from the audience and throwing the most elaborate party in the world. Mark my words, as this bowl of tuna is my witness, I will be standing up and cheering at my son, Daniel's, graduation. I may even bake a cake."

"You don't bake, Mom," I said.

"I know. But I will for graduation. Or maybe I'll just get one of those really awesome store cakes."

I push the bowl away. I fix my eyes on the merchants down the street, who are adjusting their displays, to distract myself from the memory, from the failure of it to become reality. I stare so long that the things in front of me become blurry, as if I'm watching all the shopkeepers and food sellers from behind an antique camera while their lives pass by in sepia tone. Whatever pettiness I felt last night at being left out of the *Personal* pile has dissipated here at the fish market. Because now I'm just back to missing her. It feels embarrassing to admit that. I'm a guy; we're supposed to be tough, strong. We're not supposed to miss our mommies.

But damn if I don't miss her. Damn if I don't miss having dinner with her, talking about the little things, like what app I just downloaded on my phone and whether I thought she'd like it too, or the bigger things, like what if I didn't make it into UCLA, or even just talking about Sandy Koufax. My mom loved that dog like she was a third child. Whenever we'd come back from dinner out, since we ate out a lot, or a school event, or one of my mom's treatments, Sandy Koufax would jump off the couch, stretch, then wag her tail and offer herself for petting.

"Oh, you are the cutest, sweetest, most adorable dog in the entire universe," my mom would say.

The dog made her happy. As for me, just having someone to talk to made me happy. Now my voice barely gets used. And so I miss her, and the silence in my life reminds me of how much.

I'm jerked back by the buzzing of my phone. I glance at the screen. There's a note from Kate. I e-mailed her yesterday, letting her know I landed safely. **Are you at the fish market? Say hi to the tuna for me! Every time I look at the clock now I convert the hours to Tokyo time too.**

I send a quick reply, letting her know the tuna says hello, and it feels vaguely comforting that Kate's checking up on me. When I look up, the hunched-over old woman is whispering to someone in the cramped quarters at the back of the food stall. I lean to the side to get a better look. It's Mike. He wears a white T-shirt, black chef pants, and an apron around his waist. An unlit cigarette rests behind his ear. I hold up a hand to wave. He tips his forehead in response, then walks over.

"How's it going, man? I remember you. Elizabeth's son, right?"

I nod. I'm glad he remembers me, that I don't have to dive into a lengthy explanation or reminder. "Yeah, I'm just here for—" I stop for a second, because I'm not sure how to finish the line out loud. *To see if I can ever be happy, or even remotely human, again. Would you happen to have the magic cure?* "To see Tokyo again."

"How's she doing?"

There it is. The point in the conversation where we all become uncomfortable. That all-too-familiar moment when I have to tell someone for the first time. Like I had to do several weeks ago with the guy at the coffee shop in Santa

Monica we used to go to, then the gal at the little pet-food shop around the corner from our house, and now here, with Mike.

"Actually she died a few months ago," I say, the words still clunky and awkward. They probably always will be. "Back in April."

Then the look. The tilt of the head, the heavy *oh*, like they've said the wrong thing. "Oh, man. I'm really sorry to hear that."

"Thanks."

"Damn, I'll miss her. You know, she was here every day when she was in town."

"Yeah, she dug this place."

"She talked about you all the time when she was here. Said you got into UCLA and that you were kicking ass at school." Then he points from me to him, and we're back to regular chatter, and says, "She even passed along some of your new finds to me. Like that band Retractable Eyes."

"That's a good band," I say, and I find it strangely cool that my mom channeled some of my music taste to the guy who served her breakfast. I find it even cooler that she talked to him about me. This is better than the *Personal* pile.

"They're awesome. Anyway, she was our favorite customer. We loved those crazy wigs."

"What was she like when she was here?" I ask because I'm hungry for more of this kind of sustenance. Apartment logistics are one thing; stories are another entirely.

Mike pauses to consider, wiping his hand on his apron. "The same as all the other times. She came here, had her breakfast bowl, talked about whatever movie she saw or book she was reading or her family, that kind of thing. She didn't seem like someone who was sick. I mean, I knew she was sick because we talked about stuff, but you would never have guessed from how she acted, know what I mean?"

I nod a few times, glad to know my memory of her aligns with others'. "Yeah, that sounds like her."

"She was always in a good mood too. Especially that time your sister came with her. Nice gal, your sister."

And there goes the pitch. Like the batter just whacked my best curveball out of the park, and I never even saw it coming. Because my mom didn't mention Laini's visit, and my sister didn't say anything either. I feel a searing pang of jealousy pound into me, thinking Laini might have been out here for my mom's treatments, maybe her last treatment with Takahashi, and that Laini was helping to take care of her. That was my role, my job. Laini didn't drive my mom to the hospital; she didn't clean the bathroom when my mom had vomited in the middle of the night; she didn't take her toast for breakfast the day after a chemo. Why did she *get* to be a part of my mom's life over here and I didn't?

"When was my sister here?" The words feel bitter on my tongue. I e-mailed her earlier in the week to give her a heads-up that I'd be coming here. But evidently I don't merit the same kind of courtesy, since she never told me when she came to Tokyo.

Mike looks up for a second. "A few months back? Maybe January, maybe February?"

"That's great," I say to Mike, but it's a lie. Because it's not great that all the women I know, or knew, like to keep secrets. Holland and the way she left, my mom and the teahouse and the temple, now Laini with this visit I never knew about. I think secrets suck. I don't like to keep them; I don't like to share them; I don't like to have them. I thank Mike and pay, and as I walk away I dial my sister's cell phone, and it goes to voice mail.

But there is someone I can see now. The man who may know everything. It's nine in the morning, and that's when doctors' offices open. A spark rises inside me as I catch another subway.

They are not here—my sister, my dad, Holland. The others in the *Personal* pile aren't here at all.

But I am. And I can go, and seek, and ask.

Chapter Twelve

The doctor is in.

Or the doctor isn't in.

Or the doctor isn't in yet.

See, I don't know, because there isn't any sign on his door. There isn't an OPEN or CLOSED sign. Or a BACK SOON sign. Or a Post-it note letting the next of kin of his former patient know where to find the Great Dr. Takahashi.

C'mon, Doc. You were like the messiah to my mom. You were the man. You were God. Where are you?

I even called him before I flew over the Pacific Ocean. I left a message. I asked for an appointment three days ago. How long does it take to return a phone call to the kid of one of your dead patients? I knock harder, over and over, as if the answers will come when it hurts enough, when I am raw enough. My knuckles are red now, worn now. And still no one answers. No one opens the door.

I'm pissed at myself that I never went with my mom to an appointment here, but she was the mom; I was the kid. It wasn't like I was supposed to go to her doctors' visits, especially the ones halfway around the world. Besides, she told me everything about Takahashi.

At least that's what I thought at the time.

I turn to leave, wishing I had a translator, wishing someone could decode all these clues. But I don't, so I walk to Kana, to our meeting later. I plan to ask her about the teahouse and the temple, to ask her to tell me all she knows. I'm halfway across the city when my phone buzzes. I pull it out and there's an e-mail from Jeremy.

I click it open. **Dude. This is Sydney. I met her at the beach last night. Guess what? She loves dogs! Who woulda thunk it.**

There's a photo of a gorgeous brunette wearing a gray V-neck T-shirt and board shorts and waving into the camera with one hand. Her other hand rests on top of a dog's head. My dog is looking the other way, but I see half her face. I laugh as I read the rest of the note.

For the record, I am not, technically, sending you a photo of your dog. I am sending you a photo of a chick.

I bang out a reply. **For the record, I am not thanking you for the photo that happens to include a head of a dog. I am thanking you for where that chick's hand was when you took that picture.**

Since I'm in my e-mail anyway, I fire off a note to Laini.

How's Beijing? Great, I'm sure. I'm in Tokyo now, and I heard you visited Mom back in the winter. That's awesome, though I gotta admit a little weird that you never mentioned it in all our e-mails. What's the story?

It'll take her days to respond. She's probably holed up in the library, translating ancient Chinese texts into modern-day Mandarin or something. She's getting a master's or a PhD at Peking University in Beijing. Honestly, I don't know which degree she's pursuing because she's been gone for so long—first college on the East Coast, then study abroad, now living abroad—and even if she graduated from one level to the next she wouldn't invite me, wouldn't tell me. She sends e-mails with supreme regularity—almost always on Mondays and Thursdays, which leads me to believe I am on her Monday and Thursday to-do lists. The rest of the time she is busy being Chinese, studying Chinese history, learning Chinese ways, doing everything to renounce the years she was raised wholly American.

I close the phone and continue my trek across town.

♦ ♦ ♦

My mom was a blogger, but she was more of an entrepreneur. An engineer by training, she developed cell phones for years, first for a Japanese company, then for one in California. When she burned out on engineering, she started a blog about cell phones, and very quickly it was read by everyone in the business. She scooped national newspapers and beat out online outlets for years because she had contacts on the inside everywhere. She crushed the blogging competition so effectively that a big publishing company offered her many millions for her blog.

"You've got to know when it's time to hold and know when it's time to sell," she told me when we went out to dinner to celebrate the sale. "That's the biggest mistake people make in business. They get greedy, and they hold on too long. They think they can get more. That the stock'll go up more. But the price won't always keep rising. So grab that chance."

A few months later, she was diagnosed, and fighting cancer became her new job.

As I reach Shibuya, I find myself wondering if her business advice might come in handy for me as I consider what to do with the apartment here. If I should hold it or sell it. I'll have to go research Tokyo real estate to figure out how to apply her business wisdom.

I stop outside an electronics store, where a salesman is hawking a TV set. Across the screen walks a cat, a silver-and-black-streaked tabby. The cat stops and stands on its hind legs, like it's holding itself up on its haunches, hands-free, or paws-free. Then a dog appears, a Dalmatian riding a red bicycle down a busy sidewalk. When it finishes, the screen switches to a water-skiing squirrel.

"Bet they don't have squirrels like that in Santa Monica."

I turn around to see a girl who's about my age. She is the most strangely dressed person I've ever seen, and that's saying something, considering I've strolled up and down Venice

Beach. She wears five-inch-high red vinyl shoes with huge straps across the tops of her feet and equally huge buttons securing each strap, then pink socks with purple polka dots up to her thighs, then a black pleated skirt with yellow lightning bolts. On her top, she has gone conservative with a long-sleeve white blouse, but over the blouse are suspenders with cartoon pink saxophones on them. Her hair is teased out in two pigtails, and she's tied purple bows around each one.

She gestures to the pink suspenders and the purple bows. "See, it pulls the colors from the socks all together."

"Right. Of course." I am boring in my white T-shirt, beige shorts, and black flip-flops.

She sticks out a hand. "I'm Kana Miyoshi. I figured you were the American boy, since, well, you're the American boy."

"That's me. The American boy. Danny Kellerman." She has a strong handshake. I notice her fingernails. Each one has been polished a color of the rainbow.

"And, just in case you're wondering, I'm not a Harajuku girl." She glances down at her clothes.

"I didn't think so," I say, because Harajuku girls are more Little Bo Peep–style. They wear big, ruffly skirts with apron bibs and buckle shoes. Look, it's not like I know anything about fashion, but when you've been to Tokyo more times than you can count on both hands, you learn these things. Especially when your mom has—*had*—a thing for Japanese fashion. "But the hair is kind of Harajuku." I point to her pigtails.

She puts her hands on her hips and gives me an indignant look. "You have to have the whole ensemble to be Harajuku, Danny. Don't make me take you over to Harajuku to prove it."

I hold up my hands, the sign of surrender. "I'll choose to believe you." Besides, it can't hurt to be on Kana Miyoshi's good side. She knows stuff I don't know. She knows stuff I *need* to know.

She clasps her hands and talks in a sensei accent. "You are a wise man, Danny Kellerman."

She gestures to the sidewalk, indicating we are to walk together. We pass a shoe store selling high-top Converse decorated with Batman, Superman, and the Green Lantern, and she dives right into conversation. "Do you like sponge cake? Because there is this totally awesome place only five blocks away." She waves frantically in front of us, as if to show me where this sponge cake place might be. "Wait. Correction. I should use the proper term. They're *shoto*. The café calls them shoto cakes! But really. We know what they are! They're sponge cakes. And, oh my God, if you ask, they'll pour chocolate sauce all over it. With blueberry jam too." Her voice shoots up when she mentions the jam, a sound that can only be described as pure childlike glee.

"You know, you don't sound like your e-mails."

"*I know!*" She says it like it's a shout. A businesswoman glances sideways at her and shakes her head as if to say, *Girls shouldn't talk that loud*. Kana gives the woman a sharp look and then hisses at her. I can't tell if it's playful or serious, but the woman looks away. Kana turns back to me. "But, you know, there's my business side," she says, tilting her head. Then, she leans back the other way. "And then there's my Kana side."

"Kana side. I like." I almost bump into a young mom pushing a baby stroller. "*Sumimasen*," I say to the mom. Then to Kana, "So you kind of run the apartment business for your mom or something?"

"I think it's safe to say I run the *communications* side of things," she says, sketching air quotes with her multicolored fingers. "Don't know if you picked up on this, but Mommy's not so hot in the English department."

"I think she speaks great English. Much better than my Japanese, that's for sure."

"Speaking of, Mr. Danny. How long are you here? And are you going to learn some Japanese? Because I think it's a sorry sin that all you know how to say is *sumimasen*."

"I know a few more words."

"Saying *arigato* doesn't count."

"Fine. It's a sin," I admit, deliberately choosing to keep the mood light, so she'll like me, so she'll keep talking, keep sharing, though it feels like playacting and it's taking all my concentration to remember my lines, to volley like this, a foreign activity for me after so many months. But the last thing I need is for her—the keeper of information—to shut down as I have. So I opt to make fun of myself. "Especially since I've been here so many times. It's totally embarrassing."

"I'm almost, like, so embarrassed to be seen with you

right now," she teases as she points to a side street for us to head down. We pass a *pachinko* parlor, where middle-aged guys in suits and young dudes in tight jeans feed coins into the Japanese slot machines.

"Anyway, I don't know how long I'm staying, so..." My voice trails off, because the truth is what difference does the length of my trip have to do with whether or not I learn the language? I know enough to handle the most basic of transactions, but that's all.

Kana shakes a finger at me and rattles off a torrent of Japanese words that make no sense. Then she laughs, her mouth wide open. I wish I knew what she said.

"I bet you wish you knew Japanese now," she says, and pokes me a few times in the chest. I think she is half-imp, half-elf.

"And I think you might be a mind reader," I say as we reach a candy-yellow door next to a window display with a pyramid full of springy cakes. Small chocolates in all shapes and sizes cascade down the sides.

But she's more than a mind reader. She's the girl who's been privy to stories, maybe even to secrets. And even though I soon learn that sponge cake drenched in blueberry jam and soaked in chocolate sauce is officially awesome, what tastes even better is that Kana says yes when I ask her if she'll take me to the Tatsuma Teahouse right now.

Chapter Thirteen

I try to ignore the nerves inside me as Kana guides me through streets I never knew existed. I try to swat away a nagging worry in the back of my mind. What if, after all this, after five thousand miles, after leaving California to search for what's left of my family, I find no more than I came with? What if my mom wasn't going for some Hail Mary Pass? What if there's *nothing* at the teahouse, and all I learn is that my mom just liked to drink tea? End of story. Case closed.

Then I'll be as empty-handed as when I left Takahashi's.

I make myself focus on Kana and what she's saying about Tokyo as she slides into the role of tour guide, chattering as we dart across a busy intersection, then down another side street. This one is quieter and filled with homes rather than shops and arcades. It's weird because I feel like I know Tokyo. I can get around town on any subway, making the right connections, getting off at the right stops, finding the restaurants, stores, museums, and all that stuff. But now I feel blind, like it's my first time here. Because I realize I've never really explored the tiny, twisty roads and lanes that jut off the main drags and take you to places you'd never find with just an address, a number on a piece of paper. They say Tokyo is laid out this way because of the wars—that the Japanese built zigzag streets that crisscross haphazardly to make it tough for invaders to march straight through the city and seize it.

At the end of one street that's more like a narrow stone path, we reach a wrought-iron fence. Kana opens the gate. I follow her, and she closes the gate behind us. We're inside a small fenced-in garden. Kana guides me down a winding path, past trees and bushes. Behind the largest tree is a small teahouse, perched at the edge of a pond.

Kana declares, "Ta-da!" with a flourish of her arm. We've reached an ancient-looking door with traditional Japanese writing across the front. "This is Tatsuma Teahouse," Kana whispers, reverence in her voice. "There's a legend that the tea leaves are not ordinary tea leaves. That they have mystical powers."

Mystical powers. That must be it. That must be what my mom believed. That's got to be the reason she came here. She *was* going for broke, just like I thought when I read Kana's letter.

"Tell me everything," I say.

Kana straightens herself, spreads her arms as if summoning an ancient spirit, and then begins.

"There's a legend that one of the Japanese emperors a long time ago had a young and beautiful wife, who was suddenly taken ill. He loved her desperately and searched far and wide for the best doctors across the archipelago to treat her. He even sent his men to find doctors in China. That's how much he loved her. For the emperor to turn to foreigners was a sign of how desperate he'd become. And they came. They came by ship to treat her. But with each successive doctor, she grew more ill. She couldn't rise. She lay in bed all day, and fever started to take over her body and her brain. She was hallucinating, talking to people who didn't exist. But the emperor loved her so, and when she muttered something about the tea leaves in the nearby fields, he went himself to search. And there, in the fields near his palace, fields that had grown only rice before, there was one single row of plants with tea leaves sprouting up from the land."

Kana gestures softly, gently, with her hands, as if she's drawing up a tea leaf from the ground. She continues in her hushed tone, and for a brief second I feel like I'm in temple and the rabbi is about to speak. "And he gathered them himself." She demonstrates, as if she's plucking leaf after leaf off a bush. "And he carried them back to the palace, not dropping a single leaf. Then he commanded the royal tea master to brew tea with these leaves. He asked for a perfect pot of tea. The tea master complied, only boiling the water until the tiniest bubbles appeared, then pouring right away, then steeping for exactly the proper amount of time. The emperor brought the steaming teapot on a tray to his wife, and he poured the cup himself. She pushed it away at first, but he gently insisted, encouraging her to try it. He told her it was the tea she'd been asking for. She took a sip, then another, and then she looked at him, and said"—Kana pauses now, reaches out her hand and places it on my cheek, like she's acting, like she's playing the part of the young wife—"*my love.*"

Her hand is warm, and her touch feels good. She leaves her hand on my face for a few more seconds as she continues. "And every day she drank more, and every day she grew stronger. And then she was cured."

Cured. Such a gorgeous word, such a painful word. The word I prayed for, begged for, bargained for, hoped for. The only word in the English language that mattered.

Kana takes her hand off me. My face feels cold. I want her hand back. I want her to touch my cheek again.

"And they were together for many years. They had five healthy children and lived long and prosperous lives. And the wife gave thanks every day for the Tatsuma tea leaves that had grown in the fields when she most needed them."

I want to laugh. I want to scoff. I want to blow this all off. But something about the way she is speaking warns me not to. And something about the way she tells the story makes me want to believe in the tea too. It wouldn't kill me to believe in something for once. It wouldn't kill me to believe in the same sort of possibility that my mom believed in. After all, she was the happy one, not me, not the black hole of a son. Maybe my mom had it figured out. Maybe the potential of getting well was enough of an elixir to bring her joy.

"And now it is said that Tatsuma leaves can cure disease when all other treatments have failed. It is said Tatsuma leaves bring a calmness, a healing to the mind and the body, when nothing else works. And so Takahashi sent your mother here. And we accompanied her. Because legend has it that no foreigner can find the Tatsuma leaves on his or her own."

Now I do laugh. I've had enough of the white-boy ribbing from my sister. "Give me a break."

She shakes her head and places a finger on her lips. A bird flutters by overhead. A mosquito lands on my arm. I slap it away. The garden is quiet; the silence is eerie. "Danny, it is the legend. You do not question it. You must respect it."

Okay. So this girl, despite the wild clothes, is traditional in her own way too.

I hold my hands up. "Fine, I respect it. Did my mom respect it? Did my mom, you know, believe in that story?"

Kana nods. "For a long time, yes. She believed in the possibility with all her heart."

I wonder why she never told me, never shared these beliefs with me. I knew she was a fighter. And sure, I know she wanted to live. But I was never privy to these deeper hopes.

"Can we go in now?"

"Yes," she says, and pulls the heavy red door open.

It's like walking into a shrine. There are no windows. The room is lit only by candlelight. Five low tables are arranged on the stone floor. Cushions in dark colors—crimsons and royal blues and forest greens—surround the tables instead of chairs. It is traditional Japanese seating. Each table has a tea set as a centerpiece—small cast-iron kettles flanked by cups without handles. Kana points to my shoes. I slip off my flip-flops and place them in a wooden cubby. Kana removes her massive shoes. A woman wearing a green kimono emerges from behind a wood door. Kana speaks to her in Japanese. The woman gestures to one of the tables, and we sit.

"Are we supposed to drink this Tatsuma? Even though we're not sick?" I whisper.

Kana nods and then reaches for my hands, one hand in each of hers. She bows her head and whispers words I don't know and don't understand. I follow her lead, bowing my head too. She looks up and smiles a peaceful smile. She was frenetic, manic energy spilling out of her until we arrived here. Now she is calm. Maybe this place does have magical powers.

Soon the woman swoops in, scooping up the tea set in the center of the table and replacing it with a new set, a steaming teapot and two mugs. She raises the pot several feet in the air and tilts the spout down. I watch as scalding liquid pours out. I hope she has good aim. I hope it's as good as mine when I was in the zone on the pitcher's mound. Actually, I hope it's better.

She fills the cups. Then she looks at Kana, and more words rain down. The woman chatters for a minute, then another, Kana nodding and smiling the whole time. The only words I understand are the last ones that she says to me, "*Domo arigato.*"

"*Domo arigato,*" I repeat, wondering what I'm thanking her for.

"She says she was honored to take care of your mother," Kana says.

"Take care of her?"

"Yes. She served her tea. Like I told you."

"But how is that taking care of her?"

Kana shushes me and urges me to drink. I take a sip. It tastes like barley. Like hot barley. What's so special about this *healing tea*?

I press. "How was she taking care of my mom if she died?" I am sick of beating around the bush. I want to know what all these legends, all this tea and happiness and healing cures, are supposed to mean. "In case you didn't know, she died. Okay? There was no cure. The tea didn't work. Turns out it's not mystical after all. She's gone. Done. Sayonara. The jig is up." My voice is caustic, the words corrosive, but inside I just want so badly to know all the things my mom never told me.

"It's not that simple, Danny," Kana says in a soft voice. "Nothing ever is."

I push back from the table. But it's not too easy to make a swift exit when you're sitting barefoot and cross-legged on a pillow. I fumble around, trying to scoot back more, but my legs feel stuck.

"Stay."

I obey, because it's easier than untangling myself from this table. But I don't drink any more tea.

"So you are here. In Tokyo."

"Obviously."

She rolls her eyes pointedly, then pats the small handbag she carries. It looks like a stuffed panda with handles. "Danny, I carry a panda purse. Do you think sarcasm bothers me?" She holds out her arms wide and smiles big. "I am impervious."

I nod, giving her a tip of the hat. "Fair enough. I'm sorry."

"Now, would you like to see the pictures?"

"Yes."

She reaches into the purse and places some photos on the table. My mom in her hot-pink wig holding up a cup of tea like she's making a toast. "I loved her wigs. All of them," Kana says wistfully, reminding me that I still have to decide what to do with those wigs—and all my mom's other things.

"Was she at this same table? The same one we're at?"

"She liked this table. She called it her lucky table."

I take that in, the idea that I'm sitting at the same table where my mom sat a few months ago. All my scoffing, all my scorn, drains away. *Lucky.* I wish she'd been one of the lucky ones. "But the table wasn't so lucky for her at all. The tea didn't heal her."

"Sometimes healing isn't about our bodies," Kana says.

The tea is still in front of me. I don't like the way it tastes. I don't like that it didn't work how I wanted it to. But luck? I sure could use some of that. I take another drink. It's not mystical tea. It doesn't bring eyesight to the blind. But drinking it again makes me turn over a new possibility: that maybe what my mom was searching for wasn't healing from the disease, but healing from the way it can hollow your heart.

"She even asked Mrs. Mori if we could take this picture because the teahouse doesn't allow cameras. Mrs. Mori likes your mom, so she made an exception." Kana nods at the back of the teahouse, and I gather that Mrs. Mori is the woman who poured the tea. "Your mom didn't have her phone, so I used my camera and told her I'd give her a real copy, not just a digital one. But I forgot! I'm so sorry. I meant to send it to you."

"To me?"

Kana nods. "Yes. The photo was for you. She said, *Danny can't be here, so let's show him the teahouse.*"

Everything I hide, everything I bottle up, is threatening

to spill over now, and I wish I could get a handle on this vicious game of Ping-Pong being waged inside me. I am jealous one minute, pierced with guilt the next, then simply overcome.

"I love it," I say to the table.

She shows me another one. My mother outside a temple. She's not posing for the camera this time. She's staring inside, and the photographer—Kana—has captured her in profile. She looks peaceful, content.

"You're a good photographer."

"It's amazing what you can do when you don't always resort to a cell phone, isn't it? I love my real camera," she says, then pushes the photos to me. "They are for you."

"So what's the story? Did you go with her everywhere? Like to the doc or something?"

Kana laughs lightly, then smiles. "Sometimes. She liked company. She liked to talk. And seeing as I am oh-so-amazingly fabulous at linguistics, I got to hang out with her."

"You mean you were a translator? I thought my mom's Japanese was good enough from her time working here and all."

"Let me tell you, her Japanese is *way* better than yours. And besides, Takahashi speaks English, you silly dork. Though your mom spoke to Mrs. Mori in Japanese when she was here." It's a weird thought—my mom was here in this quiet, Zen-like teahouse speaking a difficult language I barely know to a woman who was honored to take care of her, who let her snap photos in this place, while I was back

114

home studying Faulkner or writing essays on the Habsburgs or Hohenzollerns.

And this girl in front of me wasn't just the apartment caretaker, she wasn't just a guide who helped my mom navigate the city, like I had assumed from her letters and from her job. She was more, much more.

"You were my mom's friend," I say, and it comes out as a whisper.

"Yes, I was your mom's friend. We are both very chatty, in case you hadn't noticed. We both like to gab, gab, gab." Kana flaps her fingers against her thumb, imitating a talking mouth.

I smile faintly, but it's so strange, this look into my mom's life here, her friends here those few days each month when she was away. My mom was friends with a crazy, upbeat girl my age here in Tokyo. Then I laugh inside— maybe *that's* why she was so happy here and back in California too. Maybe Kana rubbed off on my mom.

"I'm glad you guys were friends," I say to the tea. I can't bring myself to say it to her face.

"She was amazing, Danny. I loved her. And I'm so sorry for your loss. And I'm so sorry I didn't say that sooner."

She reaches out her hand, places it on mine, then asks me how long I'll stay in Tokyo.

I shrug. "I don't know. I bought a one-way ticket, so I'll just figure it out. I guess as long as I need."

"What is it you need?"

It's such a simple question, but I could answer it in fifty

thousand different ways. Because there is so much I need. I am filled with so much want, so much need, and yet every day I keep reaching, and every day I keep missing the mark.

But the simplest answer is the one that feels so far away. To be happy.

"You said she was happy. I want to know what made her so happy when she was here. Especially since she was fighting so hard to live two more months. She kept saying she was going to hang on till my graduation, and it seemed like she would. It seemed like she could fight cancer forever. And then, bam. She got worse. And it all just happened so quickly. I thought I could handle it. I thought I was ready. I had a five-year apprenticeship for this. Plus I'd done it already with my dad. This wasn't my first time on the merry-go-round. But when he died, it was sudden and totally out of the blue, and everything I felt happened *after*. But with her, it was *five years* of hoping for the best and being afraid of the worst at the exact same time. Every single day. And then the end. It was more awful than anything I'd imagined for the past five years," I say, sharing everything, because it's exhausting holding up your own walls all the time. I can't fight every second of every day to keep all the sorrow inside. "And I guess, most of all, I want to understand why nothing's working for me. Why she was the happy one when she was dying, and I just can't seem to manage anything when I'm living."

Kana squeezes my hand tighter, and I'm suddenly aware that I have spoken more words to her, more personal words, than I have to anyone lately. To anyone in months. "That was like a monologue," I add.

"It was a good one. It was a true one too. Because it always hurts more when you have to go on. When you're the one left behind. It just does."

"I guess that's what I should have said at graduation. I guess that's what I was really feeling when I was on that stage at that stupid podium," I say, and when she quirks up her eyebrows in question, I unburden more. I tell Kana about graduation, how it went, what I said, then how I worked out after. I flex my bicep in self-mockery. "But see. At least my arms are strong."

She laughs. "There is always a silver lining."

"And the other thing," I continue, returning to her question of need. "I need to see Takahashi. She thought of him as her last great hope. That's what she said about him. I need to talk to him, to hear about how he was treating her. I even left him a message a few days ago. But I went there today, and there was no answer."

"He is in Tibet for three weeks. I got to know one of the ladies who works there, a receptionist, and she mentioned it to me. He treats the indigent for no charge. He will return in early July."

"Three weeks from now?"

She nods.

"I have to wait three weeks?" I ask again, as if the second time will yield a different response, a *better* response, because I don't want to wait. I came here to learn, to find, to know.

Besides, the answers to why she kept those particular letters in the *Personal* pile will be so much harder to figure out than the meds. That's supposed to be the easy one. See the doctor, get the details.

Bam. Done. That mystery solved.

"Which means," Kana says, returning to that amped-up state that seems to be her natural condition, "you will be here for three weeks!" Then she claps a few times. "Which also means you must let me teach you Japanese, okay, Danny? Let me do this for you, for your mother. Please, please, please, please, please?" She leans forward and flutters her eyelashes, long, fake purple ones. "Pretty please with sugar on top?"

She is frenzied Kana again. The girl who found me watching waterskiing squirrels.

"How much?"

Her eyes go wide, and she holds up a hand. "Oh no. I am not asking for money. I like you. And I want to not be embarrassed by your terrible, horrible, awful Japanese."

I manage a small grin.

"Whether you are here for a week or a lifetime, you must speak better than you do now."

"Looks like it's at least three weeks now," I say, half-resigned to the wait but also a bit relieved that I have a clear and definite reason to stay here so long, a reason *not* to go back just yet. It's the strangest thing, but even in spite of my monologue, I feel like I've been almost human for the afternoon. It's not a bad feeling at all. "Kana, you said my mom always told stories about her family when she was here. Can you tell me them? The stories she told you? I'd like to hear them."

Because that's what I really *need* most right now.

Chapter Fourteen

Kana leans forward, gesturing theatrically as she tells me about the district-championship game I won with a shutout in my sophomore year, about how I aced my advanced-placement history test last year, about how Sandy Koufax always slept on my bed, even from the first night we got her, even when my mom would try to get her to sleep on her bed. She tells me about how the four of us loved roller coasters and practiced lifting our arms in unison on the downhill, all so my mom could have a family photo snapped at just that moment. She talks about how my father taught me how to save spiders I found in the house by returning them to the outdoors rather than stepping on them, how that was one of his sweetest legacies that my mom saw in me even when he was gone.

I can hear my mom saying these words. These are my mother's words; these are my mother's stories. I know these stories. I lived these stories. But I like them more when they're being told to me, knowing my mom told them to others, knowing my mom wanted to share me with her friends here. She feels alive here, like she left a living, breathing part of herself here in Tokyo. The thought crosses my mind for a second: Did my mom leave these stories here for me? I'm sure that sounds terribly selfish, but did she plant the seeds of these stories, like she planted gardens and flowers and bulbs, so they could find their way back to me? Was that some kind of gift, maybe a legacy, she left for me? Maybe she knew I'd come looking. And maybe she wanted me to have them, a gesture from beyond the grave, a guide for me to keep moving, keep living, keep asking.

"Those are some good stories. Assuming they're all true," I tease, and it feels good to be playful again.

"Maybe someday you will tell me a story."

"Maybe. But stories aren't really my thing."

"Oh, but they *are* my thing. And wait! There's one more," she says, that smile lighting up her face as she bounces once or twice on her cushion.

"She talked about how you were in love with her best friend's daughter."

I grip my hand around my teacup and look down.

"She said, *Danny has been in love with my best friend's daughter since he was in third grade. He had a crush on her when she wore this cute black-and-white gingham dress to* school, *and he talked about how pretty she looked. And then in junior high he was always going over to her house to show her some funny cat or dog video, or she was always coming over to do the same. As if I didn't know they liked each other.*" Kana laughs, kind of a snorting laugh, and she sounds just like my mom. "And she said Holland was crazy about you."

Against my better judgment, against all my ramparts and defenses, I look Kana in the eyes, because I still want the reminder that Holland was into me too.

"She said she used to say to Kate, *They are so in love. So maybe we'll be in-laws as well as best friends.*"

We were both crazy in love, crazy for each other. That is true. That is a story that doesn't change. But the story has been told. I know the ending.

"So are you back together with this epic woman? Will she be joining you in Tokyo? Maybe flying in across the sky wearing her cape and Superwoman costume?"

I shake my head. "Nope."

"Then we will find you a fabulous Japanese girl to mend your broken heart."

"I didn't say it was broken."

"You didn't have to," Kana says.

I look at the candles flickering on the shelves. They remind me of the night I almost burned Holland's pictures after she dumped me. I had saved all of them, ordered prints of the best ones of her, including her beating me in a winner-take-all round of Whac-A-Mole at the Santa Monica Pier.

"Ha! Take that!" Holland held her arms in the air, victorious. I snapped a picture of her. And many more—her walking ahead of me to skee ball, her ordering cotton candy, her offering me a piece of the sugar cloud.

"How is it possible that you're hot in every picture?" I asked as I looked at her images on my phone.

She rolled her eyes. "Because you're in love with me. Same reason you're hot on my phone."

"Let's get a shot of you on the Ferris wheel."

Her eyes widened; then soon we went sailing into the night sky. She gripped my hand as we rose higher while the cars filled with people. I could feel her nails digging into me at one point.

"You okay?"

She nodded. "Yep."

We reached the top, the highest point on the Ferris wheel. "Take a look at that."

She kept looking down, though. She stared at her feet. I tucked a piece of hair behind her ear. "Are you afraid of heights?"

"No!"

But she wouldn't look up. The Ferris wheel stopped moving. "Take out your phone," I said to her.

I started texting her so she wouldn't have to see how high up we were. **You can see the Hollywood sign from here.**

She wrote back, **No, you can't!**

Then it was my turn. **Fine, but I can see that guy who walks on stilts down on Venice Beach.**

Is he wearing that red-and-white top hat?

Yep. There's a bird glued to the top, though. So weird.

I pretended to take his picture, and she laughed, but we kept on like that for the rest of the ride. By the time we got off she hadn't looked up once from her phone.

"Thank you," she said, when her feet touched the ground.

"Why didn't you just tell me? We didn't have to go on it."

"I didn't want you to know I was afraid of heights. It's so lame, my stupid fear of heights."

"Holland, you never have to go on a Ferris wheel for me ever."

She took her phone out one more time and wrote back to me. **Good, because I frigging hate those things.**

I laughed when I read the text and then took her hand. We walked down the path along Ocean Avenue. "Tell me what else you're afraid of."

"So you can use it against me?" She squeezed my hand when she said it, and I knew she was joking.

"Seriously. So I know. So I don't have to take you up in a Ferris wheel again to find out."

"Spiders, for sure."

"You picked the wrong state to live in."

"I know," she said as we leaned to the right so a late-night cyclist on the concrete path could cruise by. "There are spiders all over this city. All over my house."

"Know what I do with spiders?"

"Don't tell me you keep them in a cage as pets."

"Uh, no. You've been to my room. No spider cages there."

"What do you do with spiders then?"

"My dad taught me how to rescue them. Whenever there was a spider in the house, we'd shout, "Spider Alert!" And he'd arrive on the scene with a salute and a glass, and I'd go find a sheet of paper. And then he'd put the glass over the spider and slide the paper underneath. He'd carry the spider to the yard or the door, or whatever, and free it. He didn't like killing things. So that's what I do too."

"Look at you. Such an animal lover. Even for spiders."

I shrugged. "He loved animals. All animals. I mean, he wasn't one of those people who had a house full of lizards or snakes, but he wasn't the guy who stepped on spiders and killed them to get them out of his house either. Obviously. My sister was a total freak, though. She was terrified of bugs, and even though I was only nine or ten it was my job to capture and free the spiders Laini found when my dad was out of town. When my dad would come home from whatever trip he was on, the first thing I did was give him the spider count. It was this running thing we did. Then he'd high-five me and take me out for doughnuts as a reward or something."

"Do you miss him?" Holland asked as we neared a bench. She gestured to it, and we sat down.

"Sometimes. Like when I'd pitch and win and he wasn't there, or when I'd pitch and lose and he wasn't there. Or sometimes when I jump in the pool and I come up, and there's no one else there but me. But then there are days when I don't think about him. Which sucks and doesn't suck at the same time."

"If he were here, right now, what would you tell him? And not just some epic thing, but what ordinary, everyday thing would you tell him?"

I ran my fingers through her hair, letting her blond waves fall against my hands. "I'd tell him you beat me at Whac-A-Mole tonight. And I'd ask him where to take you tomorrow night and the next day, because one of the things that sucked the most when I started going out with you was that I couldn't tell him, and I wanted to, because he always liked you."

She smiled and moved closer. "I always liked him too, and I'm totally afraid of spiders, so I'm glad he taught you well. I'm also afraid of getting locked in bathrooms," Holland offered.

I mimed checking an item off a list. "Do not lock Holland in bathroom. Duly noted."

She leaned into me. "No, silly. Like gas-station bathrooms."

"Oh, well. I can totally see that. I don't want to get locked in gas-station bathrooms either."

"And cold. I'm terrified of cold. I hate snow and windchill and temperatures below seventy degrees."

I wrapped an arm around her. "I know that was just a cheap trick to get me closer to you."

"It was." She rested her head against my shoulder. We

stayed like that, quietly, as the joggers and cyclists and other late-night warriors pounded through their cardio. It was Los Angeles after all. Fitness is a round-the-clock endeavor.

"And being far away from you," she said, then looked up at me. No more teasing, no more punching, just the purest of looks in her blue eyes. "When I go to college in a month. I'm three hours away."

It was the first time either one of us had acknowledged *the thing*. The inevitable end of the summer. The inevitable end of us.

I waited for her to say more. I didn't want to admit that I'd drive three hours there and back every day to see her.

"It's not that far, though," she said softly, offering up an idea, a possibility. "I mean I could come back on weekends, right? Or you would come down maybe...."

She held it out there, and she was so vulnerable in that moment.

"I'll come see you anytime you want, Holland."

"You will?"

"Yes. God, yes."

"I don't want this to end when I go to school, Danny. I want to be with you. I don't want to be one of those couples that fades away when one goes away."

I kissed her forehead. "We won't. I promise." It was the easiest promise I ever made in my life.

"You mean it? You'll come see me?"

"Yes. Will you come back here? To see your *high school*

127

boyfriend?" I said it with a touch of sarcasm, but it was a mask for my own fears. That she'd be embarrassed by having a boyfriend still in high school.

"Are you kidding? All the girls will be jealous that I snagged myself a hot younger guy," she said, then pushed me down on the bench and climbed on top of me, sliding her hands under my T-shirt and kissing me so hard and with so much fire that I nearly forgot we were in a very public place.

But when I came up for air, I managed to get words out. "Being ridiculously turned on in a public place."

"What?"

"That's what I'm afraid of." I stood up and pulled her up with me, then made her walk right in front of me to my car, so it wouldn't be obvious to anyone else how much I wanted her. We drove home to my house. My mom was sound asleep, and even if she wasn't, she wouldn't have cared that Holland spent the night, twisted in my sheets, intertwined in my arms, my dog's chin on my girlfriend's leg all night long.

But we didn't stay together when she went to UCSD. She had no problem doing the thing she said she was most afraid of, after all.

After she dumped me, I found a lighter my mom used for candles. I brought the pictures taken at the pier to the kitchen sink and started to burn the first one. But then I stopped. I blew out the embers and jammed the pictures into an envelope that I stuffed in the back of my closet. I couldn't turn her photos, or my memories of her, to ash. She has always been fire; she has always been a flame.

And so the candles here in the Tatsuma Teahouse remind me of her. Then again, I am always reminded of her, so I find a way to shift gears.

"Your mom said you had to practice yesterday," I say to Kana. "What do you practice?"

Her big brown eyes light up. "I play the saxophone. I'm in a band, and we're playing at a jazz club in a couple weeks. You have to come! Will you please please please come see me perform? I play a mean sax solo!"

"So you play the sax, you have a panda purse, you're a crazy-good photographer, you like to talk, and you hiss at women on the streets. Did I get that right?"

Kana smiles knowingly, like I've caught her in something. "You noticed the hiss."

"Well, it's kind of unusual. Why did you hiss at her?"

She shrugs her shoulders. "Someday I'll tell you. But for now tell me more about your sister. Laini was so reserved when I met her."

My sister. All roads keep leading back to her, and I've got a feeling that Laini and my mom weren't just talking about tuxedo cats when my sister came to Tokyo.

Chapter Fifteen

When Laini was eight days old, her birth parents clothed her in blue footie pajamas, wrapped her in a thick green blanket, and left her outside a police station in the city of Wuhan. They were likely a poor couple, with few options, but they wanted Laini to be warm, and they wanted her to be found quickly and safely. She was sent to a foster family, who took care of her for the first eleven months of her life, until she was matched with an American couple—Garry and Elizabeth Kellerman from Santa Monica, California. They'd been waiting for a match for nearly two years. I don't really know the details, but I assume they tried to have a biological baby with no luck. And I'm pretty sure they didn't have much luck for many years *after* Laini's adoption either. Which means I'm pretty sure I'm an Oops

Baby. My mom would never admit this, but it's hard to dispute the evidence. I was born six years later. *Abroad.* Clearly, they weren't planning for me.

Anyway, my mom joked that Laini was so ultra-American, it was as if all the Chinese had been vacuumed out of her. Laini loved pink and Barbie and pizza and mac and cheese. But something changed when Laini turned twelve. She started hanging out with other Chinese girls more. A bunch of them knew Mandarin and had been taking classes at a school in Los Angeles. Laini asked to take classes too, and in a few years she was speaking fluently, bantering back and forth with her friends and with our dad. It was their bond, their thing. Even as she pulled away from our mom, she stayed close to him, and they often researched China together, looking up websites about Chinese culture, Chinese studies, the Chinese language.

Then she wanted to reconnect with her roots, so we went on one of those return-to-the-*homeland* trips when she was in high school.

I thought China would be like Japan, but that was shortsighted of me. You couldn't drink the water in China. Sidewalks were cratered in sections, traffic lights were ignored by both pedestrians and cars, and pollution from nearby factories choked the air in the afternoons. On my second day there, I saw a white-coated man pulling out some other guy's tooth in a dental office that was more like *that food stall*, open-air and exposed to all. So I stayed in the hotel room reading books and watching movies on my iPod. My mom stayed with me. She wasn't crazy about China either. But Laini was the opposite. She was energized by the country. "I want to do everything I can to help China. To eradicate pollution. To save the environment. To help the poor families so they don't have to abandon their baby girls," she said.

She kept going back, summer after summer. My dad would take her to China, and my mom and I would stay in Tokyo. Then they'd rejoin us back at the apartment. That's where we all stayed on the last family vacation, a few days after Laini graduated from high school. Midway through the trip, my dad had to take off to Kyoto for the day for work. He was heading up the Los Angeles office of his company then, but it was still based in Kyoto, as it had been when I was born.

"I swear, this'll be the one day I have to work on this trip. Then I'm all yours," he said to the three of us when he left us that morning at Hachikō's mosaic and headed into the Shibuya Station to catch the bullet train to Kyoto for the day.

His last words.

That evening my mom received the type of phone call that sends you to your knees. He'd been hit by a truck that came barreling down a street just as he was crossing it. His death was instant.

It's safe to say we were all devastated, but Laini showcased her sadness with constant barbs before she left for college. She was pissed my mom was working again right after my dad's death. Laini seemed to think mourning should have been my mom's job.

"How can you do that?"

"Do what, Laini?"

"Work. Just sit there and work as if everything is normal," Laini said, but that's exactly what Laini was doing too. She was headed off to college, getting on with her life.

"Nothing is normal, Laini. And you're not the only one who misses him. We all do."

"You have a funny way of showing it," Laini fired back. My mom returned to whatever she was working on, but my sister kept at her, trying to get her to take the bait. "I bet if he'd been married to my real mom, she'd miss him."

My mom looked up, exhaustion and frustration written all over her face. "Don't. Don't do that again, Laini."

"Maybe *she* misses me," Laini countered. "Have you ever thought of that?"

"I'm sure she does, Laini. I'm sure she never forgets you."

"Maybe I should help her remember me. Maybe I should find her." Laini pressed her palms on the table and stared at our mom, willing her to fight, waiting for her to fight.

"Perhaps you should. If that's what you want to do."

"Perhaps I will. Because you know what? I wish she were my mom," Laini said, then stormed out of the room.

I grabbed her arm. "You're being such a hypocrite. Just leave her alone."

She shook her head at me. "Don't even go there with me, mama's boy." She held up a palm toward me, like a running back holding off a lineman, and walked away.

Laini left for college two months later, and we barely saw her again, even after my mom got sick a year later. That's why it's so strange to me that Laini would have visited my mom in Tokyo. So I keep calling Laini until she breaks her Monday-Thursday rule and picks up.

"Why didn't you tell me you came to see Mom?"

"Why would I have?"

"Because you never once came home after you left for school. But you came *here*."

"Because there were things I wanted to tell her."

"Like what?"

"Jesus, Danny. Does it ever occur to you to just say hello? To start a conversation like a normal, pleasant person?"

"Oh, sorry. Right. I'm the one who vacated the family, so yeah, I'm the one you should be berating."

She stops, and the silence startles me. We are so good at this, at the cruel back-and-forth. Laini and I have done sarcasm and bitterness, cordiality and fakery, extraordinarily well for years. What we don't do is *real*. "I thought I had reasons," she says softly.

"For distancing yourself?"

"Yes. I thought I had reasons," she repeats. "I was wrong."

"About what?" I ask carefully. I'm thrown off by her change in tone, by the thawing of the polar ice caps.

"This is a conversation we should have in person."

"Laini, I'm not flying to China to meet you."

"You don't have to. I'm in Kyoto for the weekend with my boyfriend. He's here for research for his dissertation. Can you come meet me here?"

♦ ♦ ♦

I catch the first train to Kyoto in the morning. It's Saturday now, and the train is filled with families, with fathers and daughters, mothers and sons, brothers and sisters, and all I can think is this might have been the very train my father took on his last trip.

The same train, the same car, maybe even the same seat.

I switch to an empty seat across the aisle, just in case. I push my earbuds into my ears and zone out to music, letting the songs drown me for a while. I swipe my finger across my phone to switch to a new band, and like someone just jumped out of the closet to shout "Surprise!" there's a text from Holland staring up at me. The first time I've heard from her since I kicked her out of my house nearly a week ago.

How is Tokyo? We miss you here.

Even as I think about my family, about the way we all splintered, Holland is still the real shard in my hand, and I can't bring myself to take it out. I want to shut her out. I want to find the strength to ignore her forever and just let go of the piece of my wasted, ragged, worn-out heart that she irretrievably owns. But my instinct to reach out to her, to talk to her, to hold her tight, is too strong. It overpowers any ability I have to save myself.

As we wind south through Japan to the city where my sister waits for me, I give in. **I'm on a train now to Kyoto.**

Seconds later she writes: **I love trains. They are so...**

I know what she wants to say. They are so *romantic*. Trains make you think of movies and novels and rain. Trains are the last few hours before you're ripped from the one you love. Trains are all the ways you miss each other— wrong train, wrong tracks, wrong time.

I know what you mean. I send before I think about it, before I contemplate the sheer stupidity of letting her back in with a bit of banter, because her words on my screen are a purr, sexy and inviting.

The towns speeding past the windows...

Why am I doing this? Because it feels so good to talk like we used to, even though I know this is just a shadow of what we had. But I chase it anyway. **The rattling of the cars on the tracks...**

I close my eyes and imagine everyone on this train has disappeared and it's just Holland and me. We ride the train as far as it goes, into the night, an endless night with her.

Another text comes in from her. **Can I call you later? I want to talk to you.**

My phone is a pill, it's a sweet, seductive pill that'll trick me into thinking she's what I need, when she can't possibly be what I need. I stuff the phone into the bottom of my backpack.

A red sign flashes above the train doors. First, Japanese writing I can't read. Then in English: WE WILL SOON MAKE A BRIEF STOP AT KYOTO. The train lets me out at Kyoto Station, and it's a sleek, metal, modern spaceship. Soon I'm escaping the crowds and the streets jam-packed with tourists who snap photos. I haven't been to Kyoto in several years, but I studied the map last night, and now I find my way through the quieter alleys, the small shops and the narrow lanes that lead in and out of gardens and temples and that bring me to a walking path that runs along a stream. Off to the side looms a narrow set of steps. After five minutes of going vertical, the stairs end at a stone bench that looks out over the gurgling water below. Laini sits on the bench. She stands, and for a second I think she is going to hug me.

Then we both remember—we don't like each other.

Chapter Sixteen

We sit on opposite ends of the bench. Laini has packed a lunch, and for me she brings takeout sushi in a plastic container; for herself she has picked up pigeon lungs from a traditional Chinese restaurant.

"Shen and I go there every time we come to Kyoto," she says, as if we regularly meet and chitchat about her travels and her life.

"Shen's your boyfriend, I'm guessing?"

She nods and spears a piece of pigeon. "He's writing about Eastern art, comparing Japanese to Chinese. So we come here every now and then. He's spending the afternoon at the galleries and museums."

"And this comparison, let me guess. I'm betting he

thinks Chinese art is better." I pop another piece of *hamachi* in my mouth.

She gives me a stern look. She really should have been a schoolteacher in the 1800s out on the Great Plains. She'd have done well, behind her glasses and with her hair pinned up. She chews the pigeon meat, and just the thought of eating a street rat makes me sick.

"Do you really like pigeon lungs?"

"Pigeons are delicious." She offers me a chopstickful. I shake my head vehemently. "Have you ever had one?"

"No. I have never eaten pigeon, and I don't ever plan on eating pigeon."

"Then how do you know you don't like it?"

"It's a *pigeon*, Laini! You're not supposed to eat it."

"Just because you don't like it doesn't mean the rest of the world doesn't like it. You can be so narrow-minded."

"Yes. I'm narrow-minded. I'm closed off. That's why I'm spending the summer five thousand miles away from my hometown."

"Why are you spending the summer here, Danny?"

" 'Cause the Tokyo Giants scouted me. They don't mind that my shoulder is shot. They'll let me pitch," I say, and for some reason my joke elicits a laugh. Laini laughs with her whole mouth wide open. She has Kohler white teeth, perfectly straight, courtesy of two and a half years of Santa Monica's best orthodontia. I take some strange solace in this; she is more American than she will let on. Then I answer her. I don't tell her I came to Tokyo to figure out what to do with the apartment she doesn't want or to learn all our mom's secrets. But I don't lie to her either. "I came to Tokyo because I like it. But I've always liked Tokyo, and you never did. That's what I don't understand. Because you hardly came home when Mom was sick, Laini, but you went there, and I just don't get it. So what was it you said you had to tell Mom?"

She takes off her glasses and rubs the bridge of her nose. "Do you remember how I was to Mom before I left for college?"

"Remember? How could I forget? You were a complete bitch."

She winces but takes it on the chin. "It wasn't my finest moment. Or moments. But I didn't realize it at the time."

Laini has always been stubborn, has always dug in her heels. For her to admit she was wrong about something is nothing short of momentous. I let up on her a bit. "What do you mean, Laini?"

She reaches into her bag, a forest-green, woven, hippie-chick thing. She takes out a Moleskine notebook, unsnaps the elastic band that keeps it in place, and opens the note-book. Pressed between two sheets of paper is the ripped-off corner from a page in a spiral notebook. The jagged edge that completes the note my mom kept from my dad.

The missing piece.

Laini shows me the ripped paper, holding it gently in place with her index finger. "Do you see the date?"

I look down at the blue ink that matches the page that's in my wallet now. One of my mom's secrets; one of the clues. The note my dad wrote to her: *L—I already miss you. I will be back soon. Love always.*

"Of course. It's the date Dad died," I say, and, like invisible ink appearing, it clicks. That's why my mom kept *this* note.

"He wrote her this note *that* day. She was reading it over and over again after he died. And when I saw the note, I just snapped."

"Why?"

"Because it was the last thing he'd said. The last thing he would ever say. And he said it to her."

"Why would that make you snap, though?"

"Because it was to her. Not to me. And I was jealous. And I was mad. So I started to rip the note, but I stopped and instead I kept this part." She holds up the small section of the paper. "So I'd have something for me. Because this note brought up all these things I'd felt but never said."

"What sort of things?"

"See, you probably don't think about this because you're *them*. You're parts of them. But I never felt like I was enough for her."

"What do you mean?"

"She had you after me, Danny."

"Yeah, that's how it usually goes with second children. They come after the first. Besides, I don't think they were trying all that hard to have another kid. I'm pretty sure they weren't planning to have me," I say, to make light of things, to put us on even footing.

She sighs, the sad, defeated kind of sigh, as she leans back on the stone bench. "But I'm adopted, and you're their real child."

"Laini, don't say that word. You know Mom and Dad never said that," I say, because they never did. I was never the *real* child, the *natural* child. I was simply referred to as the biological child and Laini the adopted one, but we were both their kids.

"I know. But I felt that way. Mom never wanted to learn Chinese. She never wanted to go to China. Dad was the one who did. He was always the one who did that stuff with me. And she was never interested, so I felt like she wasn't interested in me. Just you. Just her *real* child."

"Stop saying that word."

"But I'd always been closer to him. You know that. I was a daddy's girl. He and I were just in synch always, know what I mean?"

I nod, picturing all the times she ran to him first, hugged him first, held his hand first.

"And when he was gone, I felt so disconnected from her. Like this rope that had connected me to the Kellerman family was gone. He was that rope. He was what connected me. He was the one who wanted to be part of where I came from. She never did. So it was like there was nothing for me back in the States. There was nothing for me with her. So I lashed out at her. Because I was so broken by what happened to him. And I had to make sense of it somehow. So I made sense of it by leaving. By believing that I had nothing to do with her. That she didn't care about me. That he was the only one who cared, and he was gone. Besides, I was going to college anyway. Mom wasn't even sick then, so *what did it matter?* I figured. I was moving on. To my new life. To the life I was supposed to have."

"You know that's not even remotely close to the truth, though, right? Because *she* loved both of us. *He* loved both of us. She didn't *not* learn Chinese to spite you, Laini. She just didn't learn Chinese because she didn't learn Chinese. There wasn't a reason for it. There wasn't some dark and terrible reason. And she didn't go with you on the other trips to China because *he* went with you. Because they had two kids. It wasn't a competition. That was just how it worked out."

"I know that now. I just had so much resentment at the time," she admits, and I don't know how to respond, because I don't understand how you can nurture something so dark, so twisted, for so long. We sit in silence for a minute. The only other sounds are birds chirping in a nearby tree. "And then once Mom got sick, I was already so far away anyway. And whenever we e-mailed she was always telling me to just keep focusing on college, that Kate was there and that she'd be fine. I was so disconnected from her already at that point that it was easy—and I'm not saying that's a good thing—but it was easy to just keep doing what I was doing. It wasn't till I met Shen and told him all this

143

that he encouraged me to talk to her. To let her know I was wrong."

"Shen told you to do that?"

She nods. "Yes. He's the one who urged me to visit her and talk to her. To say I was sorry. To see her and tell her I'd been wrong all those years."

"How did you know you were wrong?"

"Time."

"Time?"

"Yes. After a while I just stopped hurting so much. And when I didn't hurt anymore, I realized I was wrong to lash out at her. And wrong to take off. And I told her."

"How did she take it?"

"How do you think she took it?"

I picture my mom hearing Laini's apology. Listening to her absent daughter say she messed up. Without having been there, without having heard it, I know what my mom would have said. That it was all good, and all fine, and there was nothing to worry about.

"I'm sure she hugged you and said she missed you and that she loved you," I say quietly.

"Of course that's what she said."

I flash back to the card from Laini. It's also in my wallet.

I feel a momentary sense of peace thinking about how Laini was finally able to say the important stuff to our mom before she died—*I am glad you are my mom*. That's a gift, in a way, to be able to have the last thing you say to someone be the last thing you want them to have heard from you.

Now I have two answers for the price of one. Laini's card and my dad's note. But not just *any* card and not just *any* note. My mom kept those particular ones because of what they meant to her and for her. That card and that note mattered enough to travel around the world—good-luck charms maybe, talismans even—because they were the last things people she loved said to her. A promise—*I will be back soon.* Then starting over—*I am glad you are my mom.* Words of love. Words of happiness. No wonder my mom was happy. She knew how to hold on to what mattered, how to keep it close to her, how to let it heal her.

There's a lull in the conversation, and Laini returns to her pigeon, taking a few more bites. "Do you know why I stay in China?"

"Because you're Chinese?"

"Yes. And no. I came to China because I want it to be beautiful and healthy. Because I want to help the people. I'm glad now that my birth mom gave me up, but I want the families there to have a choice. This is how I make good for what I did to Mom. For how I left you both."

I want to tell Laini it's okay that she left, that she abandoned our mom when she needed her most. But I can't exonerate her for that. I can't absolve her for not being there. This forgiveness is not mine to give. It's my mom's, and she's already given it. But we *can* move on. "Are you happy?

In China? With Shen?" I ask, and place a hand on her back. This may be the first tender moment we've shared in years. The first real question I've asked her in ages.

She nods and wipes away a tear. "Yes. I am. I came to China because I wanted to feel connected to something again. And I stayed in China because it feels like home to me. It's where I live now. It's where I belong."

I don't think Laini and I are going to be best of friends. I doubt we'll be the brother and sister who hang out and catch up each week over long, friendly phone calls. I suspect we'll always be merely an item on the other's to-do list. But I no longer want to smash her guitars.

At the very least I understand her now. Sometimes that's enough.

Chapter Seventeen

When I return to my apartment, I head to my mom's room. I flick on the light and walk to her bookshelves. There are envelopes on the lower shelf with photos, and framed pictures too. I pick up a framed photo of my mom and dad. She's wearing a summer dress, and he's in khakis and a blue button-down—standard-order over-forty male uniform, he called it, saying, *I have no choice but to wear this, and someday, son, you'll have to dress like this too.* They're standing by the pool at sunset. His arm is around her waist, and you can see that her hand is curled over his hand, their fingers interlaced. She's smiling or laughing, maybe at something he said.

He always wanted to make us laugh. He used to take me out to the Santa Monica Pier for ice cream on Friday nights.

We walked past the trapeze girls and the Ferris wheel and the skee ball to the ice-cream stand at the end of the pier. We'd stand there licking cones, watching the water, him joking about something or other, teasing me about school or making fun of himself.

"I turn forty-five soon. I think I'm going to have a midlife crisis," he said over malted chocolate ice cream one night. "Should I get a sports car? Or a new stereo system?"

"A Ferrari. Get a Ferrari. Those are cool."

"Sure. No problem. I hear the dealership is having a sale. Only two hundred and fifty thousand dollars."

"They cost that much?"

"They don't call it a midlife crisis for nothing, son," he said.

But he wasn't having a midlife crisis in the traditional way, because he was crazy about my mom. He liked to sneak kisses with her when he thought no one was watching.

"You are the hottest mom in all of Southern California," he'd say to her in the hallway.

"Oh, shut up," she said.

"I mean it. I totally mean it. How could anyone be hotter than you?"

I chimed in from my room. "Can you please stop referring to Mom as *hot*? It's freaking me out."

"Let's freak Danny out. Kiss me now, Liz. C'mon, kiss me now, right in front of him." He planted a kiss on her and pulled her tight, and at that point I closed my eyes and covered my ears. He was the first one I told that I had a crush on Holland, though he'd already figured it out.

I was in third grade, and she was in fourth grade, and she wore some black-and-white-checked dress to school. It was the first time I noticed what a girl wore. Over the next few days I dog-eared all the pages in our elementary school yearbook with Holland's picture on them. My dad saw me stretched out on my bed flipping through the pages. I slammed the little yearbook closed. He patted me on the back and whispered, "Don't tell your mom, and don't tell Kate, but I think you've got good taste."

"Dad!"

"What? You think I didn't do the same thing when I was your age?"

"You did?"

He sat down on the bed with me. "Of course. Girls are great. Just remember this: manners and a sense of humor. Those are the keys to winning their hearts. Oh, and there's another thing. You have got to learn to save them from spiders. Girls just hate spiders. Like that one right there on your floor," he said, and pointed.

Then he showed me how to *not* kill a spider.

There are so many things I had to learn without him. I learned how to deal with getting sidelined from baseball without him around. I figured out how to graduate at the top of my class without his input. I taught myself how to shave. There was no dad to ask, so I learned how to do it myself.

He didn't teach me how to get over a girl who breaks your heart either.

Because last summer Holland and I talked about going to Tokyo together. She was lolling around in my pool, floating on a raft, a plastic cup of Diet Coke with a silly straw in her drink holder, her foot a rudder in the water, and she glided on over to me. I was hanging by the side of the pool, sunglasses on because it was high noon and it was bright and hot. The kind of heat that made your skin feel like it had been baking from the inside out. Plants were wilting, flowers were drooping, and the whole of Los Angeles was languishing in a heat wave. Sandy Koufax had flopped over on her side in the shade of a tree. Holland pushed my sunglasses on top of my head and said, "Let's go to Fiji."

"Let's go to Tahiti."

"Bali."

"How about the Cook Islands? It's practically off the map."

"The Maldives."

"Seychelles."

Then she splashed water on me. "Now you're just showing off."

"The Maldives? I think you might be showing off too."

"I was just trying to impress you with my geographical knowledge. Geography was my best subject. I can totally name all fifty states. Just try me."

I pulled her off the raft and brought her hot, wet body against mine. "It'll just make me want you even more," I joked, even though I wasn't sure it was possible to want her more.

150

She turned serious then. "Do you know how long I've liked you, Daniel Kellerman?"

I shook my head. "No. How long?"

She spread her hands as wide as they could go. "This long."

"That's a long time to harbor a crush, Holland St. James."

"Not just a crush, Danny. I've been in love with you."

The girl I loved loved me. My greatest dream, my most intense fantasy—Holland and me—was coming true. "Me too," I whispered as I placed a hand on the back of her neck and kissed her gently. "I've been in love with you for so long."

When we pulled apart, she had her hands on my chest, and she said, "I want to go all those places with you."

"I would take you there. I would take you wherever you want to go."

"But you know where I want to go most of all?"

"Where?"

"I want to see Tokyo with you."

"You do?"

She nodded. "Yes. Because you love it. Because it's like a part of you. The way you talk about it, the things you've done there with your family—your eyes light up."

It was like someone was seeing into me, knowing me, and I was a little bit scared but mostly happy out of my mind. "I would show you Shibuya, and I would take you to the fish market, and I would take you to the coolest shop-

151

ping areas where you could find all kinds of cute rings and necklaces and all the things you like."

"Take me there, Danny."

"You know we'd be freaks, though, Holland. I'd be the six-foot-two American, and you'd be the blond-haired, blue-eyed girl next to me."

"We'd be out of place, and it wouldn't bother me one bit. I would be a freak with you anytime, anywhere."

I shook my head, not because I didn't believe her but because I was in utter disbelief. She was the opposite of what my life had been like for years. Losing my dad, then my sister leaving with so much ugliness in her wake, then my mom's illness. She, this, us, was a gift from the universe, the thing that made it all survivable. She was the other side of pain.

"You know where else we should go?"

"Where?" I asked.

"Camping," she said, and made sure to look right at me, to connect with my eyes before she said the next part. "Because it would be my first time."

"First time camping?" I asked, trying to sound cool.

"I've *been* camping," she said, and let her voice trail off along with my thoughts. "So maybe in a few weeks we should go."

We went to this state park thirty miles north of Santa Monica, right off the Pacific Coast Highway. We walked on the beach and watched the sunset and kissed more times than I could ever hope to count. As the sky darkened, she gave me this knowing look and touched the bottom edge of my T-shirt. She had these restless hands, *exploring* hands, and she was always touching my arms, my lower back, my waist. I twined my hands in her hair, pulling her blond waves away from her face. She tilted her head just a bit, my cue to kiss her neck. Then the hollow of her throat, then behind her ear in a way that made her gasp. She said my name in this low and husky voice that made me feel as if no one had ever kissed her like this, that no one ever would or could.

A hush fell over the beach. We made our way back to the tent. We had set it up in the most secluded spot we could find, and we zipped ourselves up in it.

As soon as we were inside she pulled me against her on top of all the sleeping bags, still fully clothed, then gave me this goofy, little grin. "Here we are."

"Here we are," I repeated.

She shifted her body against mine, answering all the questions I'd never had to ask, sighing into my mouth, moving under my touch. We pulled apart for a second, and Holland grabbed the edge of her shirt, then yanked it over her head. It fell somewhere. My shirt came off next; then Holland traced her fingers across the lines of my stomach, the way she had before, the way she knew I liked. I closed my eyes and breathed in hard. Then opened them to see her unclasping her bra. She reached for my shorts, and we fumbled through unbuttoning them. I unzipped her shorts and slid them off her, and I could have stared at her all night, at the spot where her bikini underwear hit her hip bone, if I didn't want them off so badly.

I reached a hand under the waistband and stopped for a sliver of a second. She was the only girl I had ever loved, and I wanted her to like everything we did.

I wanted her to *love* everything we did.

We stripped off the final layers, and though we'd been naked together before, now there was *this*.

Holland whispered in my ear, "I'm glad I waited for you, Danny."

I couldn't speak. I couldn't respond. The power of language had been drained from me, and I was one giant electrical power line, humming, buzzing.

I reached for a condom. I asked if it hurt. She shook her head and pressed her hands against my back, and I was sure that nothing would ever be better than this, because this was better than everything. It was the real world times a thousand. It was thunder and lightning and stars.

The next day, after another time, she said, "Someday we'll do that in the Maldives. Or the Seychelles. Or Tokyo."

"Next summer," I said. "Next summer in Tokyo."

"Yes."

◆ ◆ ◆

But we're not camping now, and we're not on a train now, and we're not here now. We're not together. She's in the past, and I have to leave her there.

I think I finally know how to do that. I think I know the way, thanks to my sister and thanks to my mom.

When she rings me as she said she would, my hand hovers over the Talk button as I look at the face on the screen: Holland beating me at Whac-A-Mole, the picture that flashes when she calls. I flick back to the words I said to her at my house when I called her a disease, when I called her a cancer. I don't want that to be the last thing I've said to her. I don't want to carry a knot of anger, a kernel of resentment, that I feed for years until it leaves me scarred.

But I don't answer her call, because I'm not strong enough yet to resist the sound of her voice.

Instead I open an e-mail to her, and I take the shard out of my hand. It doesn't bleed. It barely even hurts as I say good-bye.

Hey, Holland. Great chatting with you on the train earlier. Listen, I feel bad about the way I left things. I was a jerk to you at my house that day. I'm really sorry about what I said to you. If you make it to that Statham flick, let me know what you think. Just don't tell me the ending.

I'm tempted to add a smiley face, but I don't do emoticons, so I let the words do the work for me. She'll know what I mean. She'll know that I'm sorry and that we're all good from here on out.

Then I hit Send.

I look around the apartment one more time, at all the memories this place holds. I came to Tokyo in part for a practical reason, to decide if I should keep this place or sell it. But there isn't a single bit of me that's been evaluating that choice, that's been weighing the financial or logistical implications of owning an apartment halfway around the world. And honestly I haven't thought much about the house back in LA either, but maybe that's the one I should sell, with its empty rooms and gardens I don't know how to take care of. I could find another place near UCLA, a place just for Sandy Koufax and me.

But I'll deal with that soon enough. For now I leave and head into the Shibuya night, walking down a crowded street, passing laughing guys and gals jabbering in a language I want to understand. I do a double take when I spot an ice-cream stand staffed only by a robot. Like a vending machine, but a little more elaborate. I press the buttons on the touch screen next to the blue-and-white life-size robot, and when my order has been entered, the robot shifts clunkily to a soft-serve machine, pulling levers to fill a cone with chocolate-and-vanilla swirl. As I watch and wait, I text Kana.

I am ready. To see more of this city, more of my mom's friend, more of the places and people my mom knew before Takahashi returns in a few weeks.

They have ice-cream robots over here! Can we start those language lessons soon?

Seconds later she replies. **YES!!!! Ice-cream robots rule.**

The robot hands me the cone, and I head into the crowds, keeping pace a few feet behind a loud, laughing group of friends out for the evening, coattailing onto their crew as if we're all hanging out tonight in Tokyo.

Chapter Eighteen

Before I meet Kana the next day, I reacquaint myself with Dr. Takahashi. I've Googled him before. But I want to revisit him: his work, the research he's done, the awards he's received. I flip open my laptop and settle in on the couch, clicking and searching, until it's all fresh in my mind. He was educated at Kyoto University, did a residency at Mount Sinai, then studied traditional Chinese medicine, especially herbal treatments for cancer. He returned to Japan and has practiced here for twenty-five years. He's known for bringing a rigorous mix of Western and Eastern medicine to patients—meaning you come to him for science and spirituality. Collaborative cancer treatment, he calls it. He is a scientist and a Buddhist, and his research reflects that.

I scroll through a journal article about a study he worked

on involving clinical trials of new anticancer drugs and advanced therapies, then another one where he wrote about the roles of nutrition, physical exercise, and emotional health too in recovery from the disease.

I pause at those words—*emotional health.* My mom must have been his best patient, his top student in that class. I look away from the screen for a second; it's ironic in a way. I spent the last four years working to the top of my class in school and pulled it off. I was always reaching, trying, achieving, succeeding.

But I don't know a damn thing about emotional health.

I close the computer, grab my wallet and keys, and check my phone to see if the doctor has called me back yet, if the doctor can tell me more about this hazy, gray subject I definitely don't excel at.

No such luck.

I can feel myself getting wound up, getting antsy. I know what my mom would tell me—what she always told me when I was impatient. When I was waiting to find out if I'd make the first cut of the baseball team, if I'd get that A in history, if I'd hear from UCLA—*Today, now, I want to know now, this second, if I got in,* I'd say to her.

Just be patient. Do the work, and it'll all work out, she'd say.

I do my best to channel her. *Soon,* I tell myself as I open the lobby doors and join the midday bustle and rush of my neighborhood.

He'll call soon.

◆ ◆ ◆

By the end of the next week I've learned that Kana says *ike-men* several times an hour as we walk around the city, usually when she's staring at some dude she thinks is cute. It's kind of funny to see a girl who's so obvious about it, who doesn't hide it and doesn't pretend. I've noticed she likes skinny guys with punkish-looking hair, the kind that's cut at long or jagged angles. When we meet up in the Harajuku neighborhood, weaving in and out of crowds of Little Bo Peep Girls and Purple-Haired Boys, she says *ikemen* every five seconds, it seems. Sometimes she will even tap a boy on the shoulder, say it to him, waggle her fingers, and walk away. She's even snapped a few pictures too on her *real camera*, as she says, of her favorite boys.

"This is what you and my mom did? Troll for guys together?" I ask one afternoon. Then I shake my head and hold up a hand. "Wait. I don't want to know."

She laughs and says, "Some secrets are just between girls."

Already Kana has taught me how to say: *You are a total hot babe, and I want to buy you a jelly crepe.* I don't say this to girls on the street, but sometimes Kana makes me say it to her when she gets hungry, which usually occurs when we are three or four feet away from a crepe stand. They're all over the place in Harajuku, wedged in between leather shops, techno-music-blasting T-shirt boutiques, and stores that sell tiny penguin or panda or armadillo erasers.

The only words I can get right with any regularity are *jelly* and *hot babe*, so we have created a new slang term: *jelly babe ikemen*.

Japan has different summer breaks, so Kana is still in school, but we try to meet up in the afternoons for crepe-eating and Japanese tutorials, sandwiching them between the visits she has to make to the apartments she and her mom manage. During our language lessons, we travel around the city by foot and by train, walking past skateboarders in checkered pants in Yoyogi Park, darting past the suits in the Shinjuku district, and avoiding the street hookers in Roppongi, who don't speak to me in Japanese but do talk in perfect transactional English when they say to me, "Fifty dollars for a handjob."

"Hey! What about me?" Kana says to one of the hookers.

The hooker wears tight camo pants that stop at the knee and a wife-beater tee with an American flag on it. It's a weird homage to the troops, or to being American, or something.

The hooker is unperturbed by Kana's request. She waves a hand in the air. "Fifty dollars for you too."

Kana looks at me and rubs her thumb against two fingers, like she's asking for money. I open my wallet. "Sorry, I only have a twenty."

The hooker gives us a sneer and walks away. Kana cracks up and falls against me, her black hair spilling across my chest. "She really thought I was going to pay for one for me!"

"Kana, it's an equal-opportunity world. The sooner you get used to that, the better off you'll be."

"That doesn't mean I'm buying lunch, though," she says, and she grabs my hand and we race down an alley. I don't know how she can run in the sky-high royal-blue vinyl boots she wears, but she manages, and we land in a noodle shop.

She orders for both of us. "See. I am equal opportunity. I let you pay, and I decide what you eat."

"Put a leash on me next. Walk me around. It'll work out really well."

"How is that dog of yours? Do you miss Sandy Koufax?"

"Totally."

I pull out my phone and show her the latest *un-picture*, as I call them, that Jeremy sent me. It's Sandy Koufax next to a cute redhead wearing a polka-dot bikini. Kana takes the phone and makes cooing sounds at my dog. "She is the most adorable dog ever!" Kana looks up from the phone at me. "Why don't you ever show me your friend Jeremy's picture?"

I give her a look. Her question doesn't compute. "Why would I show you his picture? And why would I even have his picture?"

"I like boys. I like to check out boys. So maybe I'd like to see what this dog caretaker looks like," she counters.

"Kana, that is *not* the kind of photo I am ever going to have on my phone. We don't do that. We don't go to the picture booths and lean our heads against each other and smile and then put decals on our pictures."

162

She sticks out her tongue at me. "You are so not fun. Maybe I'd like to date him at some point."

"Yeah, don't know if you know this, but he's halfway around the world. LA is far away."

"I know. That's why I want to go there!"

"LA?"

"To anywhere. LA. London. Montreal. New York. Paris. Doesn't matter. I want to get away from here."

"You don't like it here?"

"Oh, it's fine. But I'm not staying. My mother doesn't know this yet, but I'm *not* applying to any colleges here."

The waitress delivers our noodle bowls, and Kana and I say *arigato* in unison.

"Why?"

She waves her hands in the air as if the space around her is compressing, as if she's claustrophobic. "Japan is wonderful, but it is very traditional. And some of the people here can be very judgmental. I don't like that. I don't like that at all."

"How are they judgmental?"

"Well, don't know if you noticed, but I don't have a dad," she says as she breaks apart her chopsticks. I brace myself for a heavy conversation, and I'm almost afraid to ask what happened, but she answers before I can ask. "It's nothing bad. I mean, I never knew him. My mom's a single mom."

"You mean..." I let my voice trail off as I dig into the noodles.

She nods and sings out in a faux-cheerful voice. "Yep. Daddy knocked up Mommy and then left her. Bye-bye!"

"So you've never known him?"

"Never. They were teenagers. My mom's only thirty-four. She had me when she was seventeen. But people here—the kids at school—they look down on me because of it."

"Are you serious? Because I just kind of figure most people have weird family stuff going on."

"That's my point! But Japan can be very traditional. They don't like you marrying outsiders. They don't like you leaving. They don't like you not being like them. And literally everyone I know at school has a mom and a dad. And I'm the freak who just has a mom. A *young* mom at that. Can you believe that? Crazy! They're crazy." She says the last part as if she's mocking the other kids, but underneath I can tell it's her shield; it's the way she makes sense of her life.

"So where are you applying to college?"

"NYU. Berkeley. Northwestern. University of London. McGill. Paris-Sorbonne."

"That about covers it."

"I'll go anywhere. Anywhere but here." There's sadness in her voice. Wistfulness. "That's why I like hanging out with you," she says, cheering herself up quickly.

"But I love it here."

"I know, I know. It makes me like Tokyo more, seeing it through your eyes. Besides, you're a freak too."

I laugh, then remember how Holland and I talked about

being *freaks like us* here in Tokyo. Holland replied to my e-mail from the other week. Then sent another one too. But I've been deleting the notes without reading. I don't trust myself enough not to cave if I see her words, so I trash her messages before I even look at them, before the words seduce me into a reply. The pills I take every morning in the apartment—*my* apartment—as I look out the window at the busy streets below help. They're like vitamins; each daily dose gives me strength to keep moving on. They're a protective coating to help me stay the course. Or maybe Kana is the armor. Maybe she is my Kevlar vest.

I point a chopstick at her. "Speaking of freaks, I seem to recall you promised to tell me why you hissed at that woman the day I met you."

"Ah, good question, my student."

I shake my head, but I'm smiling.

"Whenever someone looks at me funny, I give it right back to them," she answers.

"By hissing?"

She hisses again, sibilant and slithering. "Say it. Say I have the best hiss in all the world."

"Nobody hisses better than you, Kana. Nobody, nobody, nobody."

"That's why I started dressing like this too," she adds. "To own it. To own the fact that I already stand out at school."

"Really?"

She's smiling and nodding. "Everybody already thought

I was some sort of freak. So why not just go wild? I don't have to impress anyone by being a prim and proper school-girl. So I dress for myself. I wear the things everyone wants to wear but is afraid to because of what people might think. Besides, it's pretty hard to be unhappy when you're carrying a panda purse and wearing a pair of boots that a drag queen would drool over."

The other day she wore a white petticoat, orange tights, and a yellow tank top with an illustration of a lollipop on the chest. Another time a red, white, and blue cheerleader outfit with black combat boots. It makes sense now why she dresses so wildly; not for show but for sanity. Fashion makes her happy.

And, sure, I'm happy in the moment with her friendship. I like her teasing, her hissing, her wise old soul. I like the way I feel as if I've known her my whole life and the way I feel steady with her. Most of all, I like that I *feel* alive, I feel good, I feel that thing my mom was said to have felt— *happy*—for more than just a few seconds at a time. But is that enough? I can't take Kana back with me to California; I can't hold her in front of me like a shield for the rest of my life. I have to find a way to be happy even when she's not here. I have to keep seeking out the answers, and I know they won't just be found in language lessons and crepes, much as I enjoy both of those.

"Kana, will you show me the temple my mom went to when she was here? I need to see more. I need to connect with her," I say, and I couldn't feel more exposed than I do right now as I say these words aloud for the first time, as I blatantly, patently, ask for help. Asking for more, even when she has given so much already.

But this is Kana. She does not take advantage. She does not keep score.

"It would be a complete honor."

We leave the noodle shop and head down the nearest subway steps and onto the next train. The doors close, and we're whooshing through the tunnels underneath Tokyo. Kana's hand is right under mine since we're sharing the same strap. She notices, shrugs playfully, and then shifts her hand deliberately so it's on top of mine. It's not a romantic move; we don't have that sort of chemical attraction. But as she laces her fingers through mine, I make room for them and then squeeze her hand back.

We let go of each other's hands when we reach our destination, a working-class district. We walk past several shopping alleys with tented stalls catering to the locals. They're selling staples, like pots and pans and lotions and towels.

The temple is at the end of the pedestrian shopping way—it's clearly a temple, with lanterns and a pagoda-style design, but it's smaller than the other temples I've seen and needs a new coat of paint. I walk in with Kana. Incense burns, and candles flicker. My eyes adjust to the lower light in here. I take a deep breath, expecting to hear a voice, feel a presence, something.

Instead Kana whispers. "Do you consider yourself religious?"

I shake my head. "Agnostic Jew."

Though cultural Jew would be more like it. I like bagels and lox, I crave matzo brie when I'm sick, I eat noodle kugel on Rosh Hashanah, and I think rabbis are the closest there can be to wise men. I did a year of Hebrew school, but I wasn't even bar mitzvahed. My parents were Jewish, but they both lost interest in the maintenance of the religion, and I have to say I'm glad neither one of them insisted on sending me to Hebrew school after that one year. I'd rather have been playing sports or reading books, so that's what they encouraged. I never felt like I was missing anything, to tell the truth.

But maybe I *was* missing something. Maybe if I were more religious, I could deal with my parents being gone. I could believe they were in a better place, maybe even back together again. I think they'd both like that. My mom missed my dad a ton, and if there is a heaven, or an afterlife, or *something else*, I have no doubt he'd have been pining for her the whole time until she arrived a few months ago.

Then I realize: This is the first time I've thought of them together. The first time I've imagined them as anything but ash. Maybe all I needed was to go to a temple.

Or maybe I'm losing my mind.

"I think your mother was a Buddhist. Or became one," Kana says.

I nod. This much I know about her. Not that she became one, because she didn't convert or anything, because you don't really convert to Buddhism. But over the last few years, she definitely felt more affinity for Eastern religions and for the central beliefs of Buddhism—reincarnation, nirvana, wisdom, karma, and enlightenment—than she felt for Judaism. Though honestly, the religions aren't that different at the core.

She talked about Buddhism a couple times over our many dinners out in Los Angeles—at the Indian buffet around the corner or the nearby taqueria that had twenty different kinds of salsa, including pineapple and mango, her favorites, or even Captain Wong's—no MSG, brown rice, just veggies for her.

"I sent in my application today," she said over broccoli.

I raised my eyebrows in question.

"For Buddhism. I hope I filled out the form correctly. I want to see if they'll accept me," she said.

"Ah, I hear it can be quite rigorous."

"They usually get back to you in a few months, but I filed it early decision, so I think I'll hear sooner."

"Well, that's binding, you know. Are you ready for that kind of commitment?" I teased as I speared a piece of pepper steak.

"*U.S. News and World Report* ranked it top among world religions, so I think I'll be okay with the decision," she said, then took a bite of her broccoli. Her tone shifted then; she became not so much serious but heartfelt. "I think it would give me peace, though, Danny. With everything."

"Sure. Peace is good. Who doesn't like peace?" I said, doing everything *not* to change the tone in my voice, doing

169

everything to keep the conversation light. "And I like this pepper steak. We should come to Captain Wong's for graduation dinner. Don't you think?"

She gave me a small smile, then a nod, and kept eating.

I wasn't really sure what I thought about Buddhism then, or now, to be honest. Besides, I'd always assumed that as Jews—cultural or otherwise—we were on the same page with the whole no-traditional-afterlife thing, but maybe my mom started to believe in more.

"What do you think she'd be reincarnated as?" Kana asks in her soft voice, her Tatsuma Teahouse voice.

I am tempted to make a joke, but when I flash back on the conversations with my mom over dinner, I know now's not the time to be flippant. Besides, when Kana looks at me with those earnest eyes, I can tell she is paying respects, that this is how she honors the dead. So I give the question space, and I give myself time to form a real answer. Not just words I pluck from thin air because they happen to fit the question. But an answer from within. Because I *know* the answer, deep in my gut. "A lilac bush. She would be reincarnated as a lilac bush. And she would love it. She loved lilacs like it was a religion. She said nothing smelled as good as a lilac bush. Whenever she saw one, she'd stop and smell it. And not just smell but inhale it, ingest it."

She did that at our neighbor's house in Santa Monica. When we went for walks, she'd glance behind us, survey his yard, and then she'd grab my hand and we'd rush over to his prize lilac bush. She'd lean in, breathe it, and then waft it toward her with her hand. That's why I stole clippings of it for Mother's Day that year.

"Ah, heaven," she said. She sniffed it one more time for good measure. "Someday I will have a yard full of lilacs. Someday I will spend my days doing crossword puzzles and smelling lilacs. And my children will bring me dark chocolate on a tray while wearing little waiter suits."

Then she punched me lightly on the arm and said, "C'mon, we have to get out of here before the crazy man shows up."

Kana's eyes sparkle as she listens to the story, little glimmers of light dancing across her pupils.

She places her hand on my arm. "Danny, Mr.-Stories-Aren't-Really-My-Thing-Danny. *You* just told me a story. And I think that is the most animated you have been since I met you."

"Why do you think she was so happy here, Kana? You spent time with her when I couldn't be here. What was she like? You said in your note how she was always joyful."

"I think it takes a very special person to find the joy in everyday life. Your mom was like that. She was one of those people."

Everyday life. I flash back over the last week with Kana. Crepes and conversations. Panda erasers and pictures of my dog. And talking. So much talking. About everything and nothing. Maybe that *is* enough to be happy. Maybe it'll be enough for me.

But how do you find joy in *everyday life* when you're

dying? I have a hard time finding it, and I'm the one still living.

"Let's go outside and see if there is a lilac bush," Kana says.

"I don't think lilacs grow in June."

"No, but that's the point. Maybe there is a lilac bush even if there isn't supposed to be one. You know what I mean?"

I don't laugh or snort or scoff. Because I do know what she means. And even though we don't find a lilac bush on the grounds of the temple, I have to admit I do smell something like lilacs in the air. Maybe my mom has been reincarnated here. Maybe this is her first reincarnation, as the scent of her favorite flowers.

She would like that. *I* would like that. And somewhere, deep inside me, I believe it too.

I believe.

Chapter Nineteen

June melts into July, and a sticky heat sinks down on the city. It is hot beyond words here, the sweltering-city kind of heat. The streets radiate fire, and the sun throws it right back down again, like it's casting bolts of heat, pelting endless blankets of scorching air. Cities are the worst places to be in hot weather.

I miss my pool. I miss the shaded sections of my backyard. I miss sitting under a tree and stretching out in the shade and reading a book and feeling the breezes from the nearby ocean drifting by. I miss the ocean. I miss throwing tennis balls to my dog as she fetches them in the waves.

I miss my dog.

June was a temptress, a tantalizing geisha with a come-hither wave and a dance and a sway of the hips. But July, with this heat, is her cruel stepmother. On a particularly hot Saturday morning, I stay inside where it's cool. I Skype with Kate. She reviews several outstanding estate matters with me. Things about accounts and money and time periods when I can access certain funds.

Then she takes off her glasses, and it's strange, this all-too-familiar gesture of hers viewed through a computer screen. "What did you decide to do about the apartment?"

The question jars me for a moment. It's what I thought I came to Tokyo for. To see this apartment again, to decide if I should keep it. But I've barely *had* to think about the decision because there's no way I'd sell it.

"Keep it," I say, and Kate tells me about the paperwork and details we'll need to work it out. I nod and say yes to it all, knowing I'll do whatever I need to do to keep this home as my own.

"And at some point, maybe not today or tomorrow, but at some point, you should think about what to do with the house over here."

It's so weird to think this is my decision. That at age eighteen, when I haven't even set foot in a college classroom, let alone an office for a job, I'm being asked to make this choice.

"I don't know yet," I say, but I know where I'm leaning on this.

"What about your mom's things, Danny?"

I close my eyes for a second. My chest feels tight.

"Her clothes. Her wigs. Her books," Kate continues.

"Donate them," I answer quickly, so I don't have to think about it. Then I have a better idea. "Everything except the wigs. Can you send the wigs here?"

She laughs. "For you? Something you want to tell me?"

"Yeah. I started a drag show in Roppongi. No, they're for Kana. She'll love them."

"I'll send them along with my rug. I have an antique rug traveling to Tokyo next week by private jet. This client of mine owns property in both LA and Tokyo, and her own private jet!"

"That's the only way to travel. Or so I'm told."

I'm about to say good-bye when I remember I picked up something for Kate. I hold up a plastic mackerel for her sushi collection. "And I'll send this along to you. But not by private jet. Just regular mail."

After I turn off the computer, my cell phone rings.

It's a local number, but it's not Kana, and there's only one other person I've been hoping to hear from in Tokyo.

I nearly pounce on the Talk button to take the call from the doctor's office. It's not even the receptionist. It's Dr. Takahashi himself. My pulse is rocketing, and I'm all raw nerves as he says words like *doctor-patient confidentiality* and *I don't typically do this.*

Then the next words come, and they're fucking beautiful. "But I understand this is important, and for you I can step outside the bounds."

"Thank you, Doctor. Thank you so much," I say, and I'm overjoyed that he's taking pity on me. Funny, how pity was the thing I never wanted from Holland, but it's the thing I'll happily take from the last great hope.

♦ ♦ ♦

I race to meet Kana at our rendezvous spot near Yoyogi Park to tell her the good news. Takahashi is back from Tibet, and he will see me at the end of the week. The last piece, the last thing I came for. He can finally tell me what's behind door number three.

"It's like a pronouncement, Kana, like I've been granted an audience with the king," I say, and I feel as if I can exhale, as if I've been holding my breath for this meeting.

She beams and raises her right arm straight, then speaks in a deep voice. "King Takahashi will see you now, Danny Kellerman." Then she surprises me by imitating me, adopting some sort of exaggerated California boy drawl and making a hang-ten gesture. "Dude, so it is written, so it shall be."

All I can do is roll my eyes, because she has schooled me, beaten me at my own game of Occasional Sarcasm.

When I return to my building, a blast of cold air greets me in the lobby. I will say this: Tokyo does air-conditioning well. It's arctic inside my building, and it is epic. I consider myself something of an expert in air-conditioning. I have studied the fine difference in degrees, have meditated on sixty-eight degrees as the perfect cooling temperature compared to sixty-seven degrees. I have contemplated whether sixty-six is icebox frigid enough for me. And I have declared sixty-five to be my nirvana, so I crank the thermostat to that perfect temperature when I arrive upstairs. The familiar whirring of the machine begins, a comforting hum that will usher in the igloo effect. But the temperature doesn't drop. The air isn't any cooler.

Crap. My apartment will be a sauna in minutes if I don't fix this. The air-conditioning unit is in a utility closet in the main bedroom. I open the door to my mom's room, then to the closet, then I inspect the unit, popping off the cover easily. Right away I can tell the filter's a mess, all dirty and clogged, and that's why the air isn't cooling down. It's an easy fix, so I head back to the kitchen, grab the garbage can, and return to the bedroom. I find the extra filters right next to the machine—sending a silent thanks to Kana and Mai, because no one ever has filters when you need them, unless it's your job to stock them—so I swap in the new one, tossing the old one into the trash. I put the cover back on and close the closet door. My dad was handy; he taught me to be handy too. I glance over at the framed photos of him, a reminder that he gave me this skill, that I can still find pieces of his life in me.

My eyes are drawn to the pile of photos I saw the other night on the lower shelf, next to the framed photo I'd been looking at of my mom and dad. I reach for them just to see what's there, to see what photos never made it to frames. I flip through them. Mostly they're doubles of ones that are already framed or they're the bad shots—the ones with red eyes or the blurry ones or where the subject is out of focus. I'm about to toss them back onto the shelf when an image catches my eye. I'd recognize that hair anywhere. A lock of light blond hair, the slightest wave to it. It's Holland; she's barely in the frame at all, just the edge of her hair. She's holding a white blanket wrapped around something. A throwaway photo, a mis-shot. But where's the real one? Where's the one that matches this, the one that tells the story this photo isn't sharing?

I check out my mom's shelves. I don't see it. There are no framed photos of Holland. I look behind books. Still nothing.

What the hell? Why does my mom have a picture of her like that? Not a pose or a headshot or a vacation pic but a moment in time instead. I scan my mom's desk. There's not much on it, just some Post-it notes and pencils for her crosswords, some worn down, some sharpened. There's a crossword-puzzle book off to the side of her desk. Something white, like a piece of white cardboard, is poking out the side. I grab the book and reach for the cardboard. It's a stiff photo frame, not metal but the cardboard kind that stands open, with two photos in it. My hands tremble as I open the frame.

Two pictures. In one Holland is looking at the camera and smiling. There are machines nearby, and she's holding something in her arms, wrapped in that white blanket, and a few tufts of brown hair poke out from the blanket. In the next photo, she's turned the bundle around, and inside the bundle is a tiny baby. The baby's eyes are open, and Holland is kissing the baby's head. Holland looks tired but happy.

My heart ricochets out of my chest and collapses on the floor when I read the name my mom has written.

Sarah St. James.

Sarah's not a friend from college.

Sarah has Holland's last name.

And a date of birth.

Six months ago.

Chapter Twenty

I stumble out of my mom's room.

Six months ago Holland had a baby.

Sarah is six months old.

I fumble around for a Percocet. I find them on the coffee table. I take one. Then another. I leave. I pace through the streets of Shibuya, past arcades, past shops selling socks with hearts and rainbow stripes, past pachinko parlors where people are winning cat erasers and manga figurines. How can people want cat erasers and manga figurines at a time like this? I march past cell-phone stores and crepe dealers and a nail salon advertising decals of suns and moons and flowers, and I don't understand how a nail salon can advertise suns and moons and flowers when there are too many things that don't make sense.

Beads of sweat drip from my forehead. I wipe a hand across my face. My hand is slick. I reach for the bottom of my gray T-shirt and wipe my face with the fabric. But the sweat starts again, and when I look up at the time and the temperature outside the Bank of Tokyo, the red flashing sign blares ninety-seven degrees at one in the afternoon. That means it's nine at night yesterday in Los Angeles.

I'm in front of a towering department store, eight floors high. A skinny Japanese woman in heels and a suit leaves, and a jet of cool air follows her. It's an igloo inside. I need the igloo effect right now, so I take the escalator to the basement, a massive expanse of gourmet food shops and stalls selling European chocolates and *bento* boxes and fresh fruit for sky-high prices. The cool air sucks the heat off of me, and by the time I pass the pickled radishes and eggplants being sold by Japanese women in beige dresses with white caps like nurses wear, I'm able to take my phone from my pocket.

She answers on the second ring, and I hate that the sound of her voice takes my breath away. I am fighting a losing battle with her, drowning on dry land at the sound of her saying my name.

"Danny."

I don't bother with small talk. "Who is Sarah really?"

She stumbles on her words. "What do you mean?"

"I mean: Who. Is. Sarah? Why do you wear her name around your neck? Who is she? Where is she? Because I don't think she was your friend at school. And I don't think she died," I say as I walk past a young guy trying to sell me a sake set. I hold up a hand, my palm a stop sign to his peddling.

"Who do you think she is, then?"

I pass gift boxes of cherries and Asian mushrooms while her voice weakens across the phone line, across the distance from Los Angeles to Tokyo. "Your daughter." A pause. What do I say next? "What the hell, Holland?"

Holland doesn't say anything. I try to picture her. Where is she? At her house? At the day camp where she works?

"Did you give her up for adoption?"

"No."

I stop walking. I place a hand on a counter to steady myself. There are red-bean pastry balls under the glass. No one asks me if I want to buy some. Everyone who works here can tell I'm not here to buy red-bean pastry balls. "You didn't? You didn't give her up for adoption?"

"No. I didn't give her up."

"Did she die?"

"Yes. She died." I shift my stance, move away from the food, and lean back against a section of the brick wall. I look down at the gray concrete floor. "Shit, Holland. Why didn't you tell me?"

No answer.

"What happened?" I ask softly.

"I went into labor when I was five and a half months pregnant. I was twenty-six weeks along. The baby was born premature. She was two pounds and one ounce and she was perfect in every way, except she was so small and she wasn't supposed to be born yet. She was in the NICU for two days and she got an infection and she wasn't strong enough to fight it off and she died."

The words are heavy, rehearsed, like she's said them before. I wonder if she has, and who she's said them to, or if she's just rehearsed them in her head, so she can get them out without choking on every single awful word, because they are awful, all of them, strung together like little grenades.

"God," I say, but when I try to think of the next word, the next thing, I come up short. "Were you going to keep her?"

"No. I don't know. Maybe. I hadn't decided."

"Does your mom know?"

"Yes. Everything. I told her when I was, I don't know, four months along. My dad never knew."

"But my mom knew. She has a picture, Holland. Do you know that?"

No answer.

"Why does my mom have a picture of your baby, Holland? Why does my mom have a picture of Sarah?" I know the answer. There is only one answer. But the answer is so surreal, so foreign, so completely messed up. "Was she… Was Sarah…" I trail off. I can't get *mine* to come out of my mouth. My tongue is tied.

Holland unties it with her answer. "Yes. She was yours."

Forget the grenade. It's like a dirty bomb exploding in my chest, shrapnel everywhere. I have so many more questions now that I know *that* answer, but I'm picking metal and glass out of my skin. And my voice is gone, it's shot, my throat is dry and my lungs are closed and the food stalls fade, the counter is gone, the ladies in their beige dresses disappear, and I have been blasted back to some primordial state where I don't have speech, I don't have arms and legs and voice. I sink down to the floor of the department store basement, as people, so many people, an endless stream of people, walk past me.

"Danny."

Holland is saying my name. She may have been saying it for seconds, minutes, years, eons. I focus again. The floor is concrete again, and the counters are full of food again, and the workers have shape again.

"I'm here."

"I'm sorry," she whispers into the phone. "I'm so sorry."

Sorry? Is that what this is about? Sorry? There are so many more things to be said than *sorry*. They all start with *Why. Why didn't you tell me? Why didn't you say anything? Why am I finding out now that I was a father? Why am I finding out now the kid died?*

That blasted feeling returns, like the bomb Holland lobbed has ripped out my organs. I don't even know how I'm supposed to take this, receive this, accept this, deal with this. I don't have a clue. You would think I'd be an expert, a professional griever at this point. That this would be second nature. That this would be my best subject, the class I excel at.

But the only thing I feel for sure is a sick form of relief. I'm eighteen years old. I'm about to start college. I don't have a family. I'm the last person in the world who should have a child. The girl I love has been broken to pieces by this for the better part of a year, and I never knew it. But me? All I can think is, *Thank God I don't have a kid.* I have dodged a bullet, one that was heading straight for my head.

I can't say this to her. I can't say this to anyone. A family walks past me. The mom glances over. She knows. She looks at me, and she can tell. I am a boy who had a kid he didn't want, and the kid died, and there's a part of him that's glad.

How did I become this person? I do not like this person. "I can't believe you didn't tell me. I can't believe you didn't ask me what to do. I can't believe you didn't say a word. Then or ever."

"I have been wanting to tell you for the last few weeks. Why do you think I e-mail you all the time? Why do you think I called you?"

"I don't know. How am I supposed to have a clue?"

"I have been trying to explain everything."

"You want to explain things? You want to explain things now? That sounds great. Why don't we meet for coffee tomorrow, and you can tell me everything you've been try-ing to explain?" Then I hang up on her.

I drop my head between my knees, but I don't think it's Holland I'm mad at for not telling me. I'm mad at someone else. Someone I've never really been mad at before.

My mom.

Chapter Twenty-One

Holland worked at a camp every summer during high school, but it never seemed like work for her. She had a natural connection with kids. One day last year, I picked her up from camp, and she was sitting at the picnic table in front of the school where the camp was held. There was a little girl with her. Her parents must have been late picking her up or something, so I joined them at the bench, and Holland and the girl played tic-tac-toe for probably twenty minutes. The girl beat Holland in a round and did a little jig, then Holland beat the girl and held her toned arms up in the air victoriously. It went on like that—sometimes Holland let her win, sometimes Holland won purposely, and sometimes it was a draw.

I liked that Holland didn't just let the kids win all the time. I liked that she was playfully competitive with them.

"You know tic-tac-toe originated in Egypt?" Holland said to the girl.

The girl shook her head. "I don't think so."

"Maybe it was Madagascar then?"

Another head shake.

"Okay, I'm thinking Romania."

The girl started laughing. "No! Not Romania."

"Well, where then? Where do you think tic-tac-toe originated?"

The girl shrugged her skinny shoulders. "I don't know."

"We should find out. We should research it. Can you look it up tonight?"

"I don't know how to do that!"

"Just Google it and get back to me. Maybe write a report. Can you do that for me?"

The girl laughed more and shook her head. "I don't know how to do a report, Holland!"

"Well, maybe you can just make me some chocolate chip cookies tonight. No, wait. How about cupcakes? Can you make German Forest Tree Frog cupcakes?"

"I don't think you want to eat tree frogs."

"No? I heard they taste great with chocolate icing. Doesn't everything taste better with icing?"

"I love icing. What if cupcakes were just made of icing?"

"What about icing and Skittles?"

"That would be messy."

"But good. Don't you think?"

The girl nodded. "How much does my mommy owe you?"

Holland looked at me. "Late pickup fee," she explained.

When the mom showed up, she was frazzled, harried, and her hair was unkempt. She dug through her purse for a checkbook but didn't have one.

"I'm so, so sorry," the mom said.

"It's nothing," Holland said, and waved a hand in the air. "We had fun."

"I'll pay you tomorrow, I promise."

"Seriously. Don't think twice about it. It's on the house."

The mom left, and we invented scenarios as to why she was late as we drove away.

"She was stuck in traffic," Holland suggested.

"No. She was getting her nails done."

"Botox, baby. She was getting Botoxed."

"Tummy tucked."

"Dolphin tattoo on her butt."

"Nipple pierced."

"Ewww!" Holland said, and wrinkled her nose.

"Belly button pierced?" I offered.

"Much better. But I think she was having an affair with her boss."

"Ah, a little afternoon delight."

"And they just came from the Beverly Hills Hotel."

I nodded. "Yeah, she's totally having an affair. But it's not her boss. She's seducing a much younger guy."

"Younger guys are the best," Holland said, and placed

her hand on my leg. We reached a traffic light, and she leaned in to whisper, "Let's pull over somewhere soon."

I found the emptiest floor at the next closest parking garage, and we climbed into the backseat of my car.

We both had clean bills of health, so Holland had gone on the Pill by then. For all I know that might have been the time the birth control didn't do its job.

◆ ◆ ◆

I turn the apartment upside down. I empty every drawer, every cabinet, every cupboard. I do it again. And again. By the end of the day, I have found nothing else. Nothing else my mom hid from me, nothing else my family didn't tell me. But I'm sure something's there, lurking.

Something to make sense of this mess. Because this does not compute. My mom didn't keep secrets like this. She wouldn't. She was honest and open and up front. When I was in third grade, the other kids were starting to talk about the birds and the bees, but no one quite got it, especially the details on how we'd all managed to escape out of our moms as babies. I asked at dinner one night.

"Mom, how did I get out of your belly?"

She laughed hard. My dad chuckled, looking away. Laini guffawed. "Oh, this is going to be good," she said.

My mom looked at me, trying to wipe the smile off her face. "Do you really want to know? Are you really ready for the answer?"

"Yes."

Then she told me. Not in graphic detail or anything. But enough to dispel my previous notion that I'd somehow emerged *Alien*-style. "That is the most disturbing thing I've ever heard," I said.

The three of them laughed throughout the rest of the meal. But even that truth didn't stop me from asking more questions over the years. I asked; she answered. That was the deal. Even when she was first diagnosed, I asked her, tears streaking down my thirteen-year-old cheeks, if she was going to die.

"It's possible, but I am going to do everything I can to fight it. I promise."

If she was so honest about all that, why then would she hide *this*?

I leave her room and slam the door. I like the sound of it, so I slam it again and again, the sound echoing through the apartment, the noise splintering in my ears.

I return to the living room, to the lilac seeds on the coffee table where I tossed them my first day here. Lilac seeds from Holland. Then the note Holland sent my mom on lavender paper that I've been keeping in my wallet. Three clues in the *Personal* pile, and this last one is now abundantly clear. I read the note again, looking at it in a new way. I *never* would have guessed what it really meant—a makeshift memorial for my mom's only grandchild.

I ordered these online for you, but they are from the Japanese lilac tree. As you know,

They take a few years to bloom, but they will produce the most fragrant and aromatic flowers. It's nice, in a way, to think about flowers to be remembered by, isn't it? And that in a few years, these lilacs will delight people with their scent. Maybe you can find a place to plant them in Tokyo?

How could they have this little secret and keep it from me? A coldness settles into my chest, a deep black coldness, like the dark of space. I am floating out there, on the edge of it all, about to be sucked into the black hole. The only thing keeping me *here* is this anger that I am encased in, all icy and frozen, as I spend another vacant night in a lonely home, far away from everyone.

◆ ◆ ◆

When daylight mercifully comes, I ask Kana to go to the movies with me, and we spend the afternoon in a darkened theater, eating popcorn and gummy bears, and the only thing not lost in translation is the food and the comfort.

But it's still not enough to right this capsized life of mine. We leave, and as we near the Hachikō mosaic, as we stand under the baking afternoon heat, I ask her if my mom ever mentioned Sarah to her.

"Yes," Kana says with a nod.

"What did she say?"

"She said Holland had a baby. And Holland lost a baby."

"You knew."

"Yes. I knew."

"Did you ever want to tell me?"

She doesn't answer right away, just tilts her head to consider. Then she speaks. "I didn't really think about telling you, Danny. I didn't know, one way or the other, if you'd ever known. And it never came up in all our conversations, and to be honest, Holland hasn't come up much either." She looks straight at me when she says that, and I nod, because it's true. Kana and I haven't talked much about Holland, and the omission hasn't been deliberate, it's just happened naturally. "So I never felt as if Sarah was something to be told, do you know what I mean?"

"I guess. But I just don't understand how everyone knew, but no one told me. My mom, Holland, Kate. They all knew, and my mom told *you* instead. And don't get me wrong, Kana. I think you're awesome, but you're not the father of the—"

I can't even finish the sentence.

"Sometimes it is easier for us to tell hard things to people who are far away. That's how we test out saying things."

"But my mom never told me. I can *almost* understand Holland not saying anything. She was eighteen and pregnant. But my mom? What's her excuse?"

"She didn't want to hurt you. That's what she told me."

"Did she show you the picture?"

"Yes. Sarah was a beautiful baby." I don't know what to

say to that. I don't think babies are beautiful. I don't think babies are anything. "She showed it to me at the teahouse one day after your sister came to visit."

I close my eyes and reach for the dog mosaic, holding on to Hachikō's white ears for a second. Kana reaches out and places a hand on my arm. I open my eyes. "What is wrong with my life? Why is everything so fucked up?"

"What is so messed up?" Kana asks as she shifts her words from my curses to her softer ones.

I don't tell her that my grasp on truth, on words, on people, has slipped. I was getting close, so close to normal again, and that's been snatched away. I'm not even back where I started. I'm somewhere else entirely, so far off the map I don't know where to turn next. I look away, at the jumbo screen on the building across the street. A Chihuahua walks across a tightrope. "How could my mom know and not say anything? She was supposed to be on my side. She was *my* mom. Why was she on Holland's side?"

"Is this a war between you and Holland? It wasn't a battlefield. It wasn't a fight. There are no sides. All sides of it are sad, okay?"

"You know what I mean."

She shakes her head. "No, I don't."

"How could my mom know Holland had our baby and not tell me?" I grab Kana by the shoulder, and she tenses for a second. I let go. I can't hurt her. She is the one person I can't hurt. I can't shake the answer out of her.

194

"Danny. Why do you think your mom didn't tell you?"

I hold up my hands. "No clue."

"Because she was dying. Because she didn't want you to have any more loss in your life. You'd lost your father, your sister was gone, your girlfriend had broken up with you, and you were losing the person you loved most—her. Your mom. She didn't want you to have one more thing to deal with. She wasn't keeping a secret from you. She was protecting you from a secret."

I shake my head many times. "No. No. No. That's not how it works. That's not how it works," I repeat.

"You have to understand she did it because she loved you. But you also have to understand that she wanted a picture of the only grandchild she would ever see. Even if that baby was already gone."

Kana puts her arms around me, and I resist at first, resist the closeness, the connection, until finally I let myself fold into her. She wraps her skinny arms around me, and maybe this, maybe her, is why I came to Tokyo. She is the only thing that makes sense to me.

She holds on to me, or I hold on to her, I can't tell, because I don't want to separate myself from her.

Soon the sun is too much; the heat is too much. No one can last outside this long in the heat of the day.

"This is going to sound crazy, but do you want to go to karaoke?"

I laugh. "Really?"

I pull back, untangling my arms from her and my face from her shoulder.

"Sometimes I think when we are sad, we need to do the opposite of sad. Sometimes we need to sing."

She takes my hand, loops her fingers through mine, leads me to the nearest karaoke place just a few blocks away, and orders up a karaoke room. She starts with the karaoke standards, Bon Jovi and the Beatles, then we hit newer tunes, Katy Perry and Arcade Fire, and we laugh and toast and hold our soda glasses high and say *kampai*, a Japanese *cheers*, and then sing more songs. We sing duets, including a ridiculously cheesy Dolly Parton and Kenny Rogers song about islands, and she teases me mercilessly because my voice is so bad, and I cannot carry a tune at all. When we flip through the Guns N' Roses section, she skips over "Sweet Child o' Mine" and picks "Welcome to the Jungle," and for this I want to buy her jelly crepes for the rest of her life. When the sadness is pumped out for the moment, we leave and head into the neon Tokyo night. I walk Kana to the subway station, and say good-bye as she cruises through the turnstiles on her way home.

I make my way through the evening crowds, the sidewalks teeming with people, and turn onto my street.

I stop in my tracks, because I must be imagining this. Imagining the outline of someone I'd recognize anywhere— the hair, the legs, the curves of the body. There's a piece of paper in her hand, and she's looking for numbers on buildings, and she's just a few feet from my building, trying to find the address that matches the one in her hand.

When she turns around, I'm looking into the most beautiful blue eyes I've ever known.

And she smells like lemon sugar.

Chapter Twenty-Two

"How did you get here?" I ask. It's a dumb question, but still it comes out, because here she is and she called me on my bluff.

"I took a plane."

"Right. Those things that fly over the ocean."

"I got a cheap flight."

"Oh good. I wouldn't have wanted you to spend any real money to come here."

"I didn't mean it like that. I didn't mean I would only come because the flights were cheap."

"Then why don't you say what you mean for once? Or is that just too hard to do? To tell the truth?"

She shifts her bag higher on her shoulder. "Can we talk?"

"Is that why you're here?"

"Yes. To talk. To see you." She gestures to the door of my building. "I came here because you wouldn't talk to me on the phone. You wouldn't answer my e-mails."

"Note to self: As long as you fly across the ocean, the girl finally appears."

She nods slightly, absorbing the blow. "Is there someplace we can go?"

"Oh, like my place? Do you want to come upstairs and have tea and we can talk there? Maybe we can even put Sarah's photo on the table while we chat. I'll get out the lilac seeds you sent my mom."

Holland looks away, swallows.

"Sorry," I mutter. "That was shitty."

She shakes her head. Her blond waves are flatter than usual. Ten hours on a plane will do that. "It's okay."

"No, it's not. But we can't go to my place." The apartment is not my house in Los Angeles. It's not a place she gets to float in and out of when she appears with food or with luggage. This place is mine. "Are you hungry?"

"Starving," she says, and flashes me the tiniest smile. I look away.

"I know a twenty-four-hour sushi place." I guide her down a quiet side street. There are no street barkers hawking TVs or cell phones here. I tip my forehead to a half-wood, half-screen door that I slide open. We enter a sardine-size sushi shop. The gentleman who runs the place holds out his arms and grins.

"*Hisashiburi*," he says. *Long time no see.*

"*Chigau? Senyoru ni kittan darou.*" *Are you kidding? I was here the other night!*

He shrugs playfully, then asks me what I want to eat.

I gesture to Holland. "*Kanojo no hoshii mono.*" *Whatever the lady wants.*

He laughs, a deep hearty belly laugh and looks at Holland, then spreads his arms in front of the sushi bar, stocked with tuna, octopus, yellowtail, salmon, shrimp, and more. "Anything for you," he says in a thick Japanese accent.

"Thank you," Holland says, and we sit down. She leans into me. "You speak Japanese."

"Just a tiny bit."

"That was a whole conversation, Danny," she says, and there's pride on her face. It makes me sort of want to flex my muscles and let her watch. Then I lose the thought, because We. Had. A. Kid. And. The. Kid. Is. Dead.

"You should order," I say, pointing to the food.

"Are you going to eat?"

"Sure." I ask for some salmon, tuna, and octopus, and she chooses eel, miso soup, and edamame.

"So..." I say.

"I saw Sandy Koufax," Holland begins. "I ran into her and Jeremy at the beach a few days ago. She raced up to me to say hello. She wagged her tail and put her paws on my chest and licked my face."

My dog. My loyal, faithful dog.

Holland continues. "I think she wanted me to say hi to

you too. So from Sandy Koufax, *hi*. She misses you." Holland stops talking and pauses. She looks straight at me. "She's not the only one."

I shake my head. "Don't."

If I let her talk like this, I will sink. My whole body will go underwater and never come back up.

"But I do. I do miss you, Danny. I've always missed you. I've missed you every day since..." Her voice trails off for a few seconds. "And that's why I wanted to talk to you. That's why I've been e-mailing and calling. Even if it took me flying five thousand miles, I'd fly five thousand more to tell you."

"What are you going to tell me?"

"I want you to know why I never told you the truth about Sarah."

"Okay. Tell me the truth," I say as our guy hands over a plate of sashimi and some miso soup. It seems strange to be eating and talking about *this*.

"You know how I love kids," Holland begins. "I love taking care of them. I love working at the camp. And I've always wanted kids. Just not as a teenage mom, not as a freshman in college, obviously. So when I found out I was pregnant, it was all so wrong." She doesn't touch her soup, just rests her hands on the counter as she talks to me. "But it was all so right in this weird way too. I think that's what surprised me the most. I mean, as a girl you always think at some point, *What would I do if I got pregnant before I was ready?* But then it happened. And I was shocked. Because

201

we were careful even when I started on the Pill. So I took, like, ten pregnancy tests. And every time, it didn't feel totally wrong. It felt like something I'd want. And with you. But just not then. So I was totally confused, and then that just turned into being totally paralyzed. Because all I knew was that I wasn't going to end the pregnancy. But I couldn't think beyond that."

"So naturally you dumped me."

"Yes."

I hold out my hands, waiting for an answer. But it doesn't come yet.

"I couldn't think beyond each moment. I couldn't tell anyone. I couldn't tell my mom or my roommate. I wore these baggy clothes, and I carried my backpack in front of me to class. And I was this zombie of a person. Just going through the motions of each day until I could figure out what to do and how to say it."

I soften my voice. "I would have helped you figure it out. You know that, don't you? I'm not some idiot who can't handle complicated stuff."

"I know." She fiddles with a rubber band, a black pony-tail holder around her wrist.

"Why didn't you tell me?"

"Because I could barely deal with it myself." There is a fierceness in her blue eyes, an intensity to them. "Because I knew if I saw you, I would have wanted to keep her. I would have been this stupid hormonal girl who was getting fat, and I'd be like, *Danny, let's have a baby. Let's play house.*

Let's get married and be teenage parents. I would have done that. I would have begged you, and we'd have been this joke. I had to cut you out because I didn't want to put you in that position. I needed time to be okay with the idea that I was going to have to give her up before I told you. I planned to tell you. I mean, I knew I should tell you. I knew that, Danny." Now her eyes plead with me. "And I talked to adoption agencies even though it broke me apart to think about giving her up. But I knew I had to. I just wanted to get my act together and a plan together and tell you when it was all sorted out. I wanted to be able to tell you without it messing up your life. Besides, I figured I'd have *time* to sort it out. I thought I could tell you when I had an adoption agency picked and when I was certain what I was doing. But then I went into labor. And everything happened so quickly. I had to get a cab to a hospital in San Diego and then call my mom and ask her to come down."

When she says that, a memory flickers. Kate being gone for a few days six months ago. My mom not even knowing where Kate went. Just that she had to take care of business out of town.

"And my mom raced down to San Diego, and she arrived a few minutes after Sarah was born. It all just happened so quickly."

"Jesus. You were alone when you had her?"

Holland nods. "I'd never imagined I'd give birth that early. That had just never even occurred to me. I never thought I would run out of time to tell you. I truly never

203

thought she'd be born before I could say something. But then they handed her to me, and I was overwhelmed with love for her. I was like this fierce lion, and I just wanted to protect her," she says, her voice strong, the look in her eyes telling me she is both *here* and *there* right now. "She was small, so small, she could fit in my hands. Her face was reddish and a little bit blue at the same time. Her eyes were barely open, and her feet were tiny, and she let out this little sound, not like one of those full-bodied baby screams but more like a kitten's meow."

She puts her hand against her mouth for a second, her voice catching. "And I knew I had to protect her, and I had to fight for her. My only thought was I had to save my baby. But I couldn't. She got an infection, and I wasn't enough for her. What I had to give her wasn't enough. I couldn't do a thing. I failed her completely. She lived for exactly fifty-two hours. Her heart had been beating, and I had held her, and she was this *real* person. And when she died, all I felt was black and empty. We didn't have a funeral or memorial service or anything. She was just cremated. That was it. And it was absolutely horrible—this tiny little person turned to ash."

I try to picture a baby, a two-pound baby, being cremated. But it's too awful a thought.

"And I thought her dying was all my fault. A punishment for not having figured out what to do beforehand."

"Holland, it's not a punishment. The world doesn't work that way. Bad things just happen."

She shakes her head. "I don't know. That's how I felt at

the time. And my body. It was just this mess. My body didn't know she was dead. My body was trying to be a mom. And how could I tell you then? How could I tell you at that point? Just call you up and say, *Oh, hi. I didn't have the guts to tell you I was pregnant, but now I'm not, and now she's dead, and I feel dead too, and can you please come save me from all this?*"

I reach for her. I don't care if she *should have, could have, would have* told me. I can't let her, I can't let *anyone*, go through this alone again, whether it was her choice or not. She presses her wet cheeks against my T-shirt, and I let her cry into my chest. "I would have saved you, Holland," I say into her hair. She nods roughly against my chest.

I touch her hair for a second, then pull away.

"I know. I know, but I was scared. Besides, you were with Trina then. Even if you weren't, what was the point? It wasn't bringing her back. Then your mom got worse, Danny. That was when we all knew she wasn't going to make it. How could I just add to that?"

I remember that clearly too. The blunt conversations the doctors had with my mom. Telling her it was time to get her affairs in order.

"How did my mom know about Sarah, though?"

"My mom told your mom after Sarah died. You know how they are. They tell each other everything. And the picture—my mom had taken the photo just a couple hours after I had her, and then after Sarah died she said she wanted to give your mom a picture because it would be the"—Holland stops, looks away for a moment to swallow, then manages the next part—"the only way your mom would ever see one of her grandkids."

All the things my mom will never see and never know flash before me. She will never know what I'll study in college, who I'll marry, how many kids I'll have, what I'll do for a living. She will never learn golf or qualify for a senior discount at the movies. She will never grow old.

Holland keeps talking.

"That's why I hated college. I hated every single thing. I hated that she died. I hated that I hadn't made a decision soon enough. I hated myself for being so weak, for not being able to tell you, for not being able to save Sarah. And then I came back for the summer, and I couldn't stay away from you."

Despite myself, I manage the smallest of smiles.

"I couldn't. I mean, you know what happened! I kept coming over and bringing you food and trimming the flowers and inviting you to lunch. And just showing up. And every time I'd think, *This will be the time I tell him.* But you were just so broken, understandably, and I just didn't want to pile on. It felt unfair then to tell you. Like I'd just be getting it off my chest and making a new problem for you. And I didn't want to do that. It's not that you couldn't handle it, Danny. I didn't want you to *have* to handle it."

"I could have handled it."

She places her soft hand on my arm. I tense but then give in to how good it feels to be touched by her. "I know," she says.

"And the reason I know that is because nothing has changed for me. I'm still totally in love with you. I've never stopped."

She's doing it again. She's saying things that make it impossible for me to be mad, impossible for me to resist. I want to wrap my arms around her, pull her next to me, and stroke her hair. I want to plant kisses on her forehead, her cheek, her glorious neck. I want to tell her I miss her so much too that the missing is like its own life force, like a living, breathing organ of fire inside me, and that I would do almost anything to take the pain away from her. But some other force, fueled by the memory of all the hurt she's caused, is pulling me the other way.

I am not ready to open myself to the fire again, to the burning of Holland.

"I'm not ready," I say to her.

She nods, taking the punch. "I have more pictures of Sarah if you ever want to see them. They're not scary or sad. They're pictures of her all wrapped up and sweet-looking in a little baby blanket or sleeping in my arms when the doctors would let me hold her for five minutes at a time before she went back into her Isolette. Maybe that sounds too weird or depressing. But I'm trying to be open about it now and tell you all the things I never told you before."

Baby pictures. This is the real foreign language.

I look at her next to me here in Tokyo. I've always wanted her *here* with me. But this isn't exactly how I pictured it. Even so, I need to say the next words to her. "Holland, I don't agree with you not telling me. But I do understand what you're saying. I do understand why you thought you had to do it that way."

Then I move on and ask her where she's staying.

"You know my mom has that client in Tokyo?"

I nod.

"She's going to let me stay with her."

"How long are you here?"

She hesitates before she answers. "A week. I'm done with the camp job for now."

I want to invite her back to my place, but I just can't stand the thought of losing someone else again.

"You should eat," I say instead.

Chapter Twenty-three

I return to the temple my mom used to visit. It is dusk. The midday heat rays have been washed away by the cooler evening air. I wave my hand through the sickly-sweet-smelling incense, spreading it through the temple. No one is here, just like the last time. But I can feel my mom in this place. I can feel that she was here just a few months ago.

I was close to my mom. I told her stuff; I leaned on her; I asked her for advice on almost everything—friends, school, girls, sports, college. I stand in the darkened temple, lit only by flickering candles, staring at a stone statue of Buddha with his hands clasped together, and I wonder if I would have asked my mom what to do about a pregnant girlfriend.

Hi, Mom. I got a girl pregnant. What should I do?
Does she want to keep the baby or give it up?

She doesn't know.

Well, son, you should—

That's as far as I can get. Because she's not here to fill in the blanks, and because she didn't tell me about it anyway. I try to imagine what I would have done if I were Holland. Who would I have told? If Sarah had lived, would Holland have kept her? Would she have quit school to raise a kid? If she had given her up, would it have been an open adoption where you stay in touch? Maybe in ten years Holland would have become buddy-buddy with the ten-year-old Sarah and then have ice-cream dates and shopping trips and prom consultations with the teenage Sarah. Maybe teenage Sarah would have wanted to know her dad. Maybe teenage Sarah would have been like Kana, wanting to fly away, wanting to escape.

But that didn't happen. Because Sarah went the way of so many people in my life.

I close my eyes and try to picture the NICU, the doctors telling a scared college freshman who'd given birth to a baby too soon that the child was dying. Did Sarah fight to live like my mom? Did the doctors do everything they could? Did they say, *Sorry, we can't save your daughter*? And then wrap the baby in a blanket and hand her to Holland to hold till Sarah took her last breath?

I know what it's like to watch someone you love die. I was there the night my mom died. It was at our house in Santa Monica, in her bedroom. I held one hand, and Kate held the other. My mom's breaths grew farther apart and fainter. Then they were rattling almost, like she was sucking in air, gulping, but only once every minute. Her eyes were closed—she was hardly there; she'd said her goodbyes—and now we were just watching, just witnessing the closing down of her body. A final inhale, a final exhale. Then the barely visible rising and falling of her chest stopped once and for all.

All that was left was me and my dog, and my goal in life became singular—to strike out anything inside me that resembled a feeling.

I leave the temple and walk around the back of the building with its peeling, faded paint. I stop short when I see a cemetery. It's not a regular cemetery. The graves are different. The headstones are small. They have teddy bears next to them and bonnets on top of them. I am in a baby cemetery. I take another heavy, leaden step and read the dates, just to be sure, just to hold my finger in the flame a few more seconds.

I have to *feel* this pain. I have to *let* myself feel it.

I force myself to stare at the headstones, to read the names on them and the dates. This baby lived for three days. This baby for a year. This baby for five months. I feel as if someone has reached a hand through my chest, a fist, and it's gripping my heart, squeezing it, wringing it, and suddenly I'm coughing, I'm choking, I'm down on my knees.

Something like tears is building up deep inside me, and I

cough some more, like I'm hacking up a lung. I have lost something I didn't know I had and something—to be honest—I didn't want. I didn't want to be a father. I didn't want to have a baby. But I didn't want my firstborn child to die either. For the briefest of seconds, I picture my mom and Sarah. Somewhere else, someplace else, someplace heavenly, where it smells like lilacs and my mom has all her straight brown hair, curly at the ends, and she is laughing and holding hands with a little girl.

Sarah is with my mom. My mom is with Sarah. My dad is even there too. Together, all of them.

My mom wanted to know Sarah, the only grandchild she would ever know. My mom took her picture to Tokyo, looked at it, maybe even touched it, maybe even remembered the girl who would never live.

And I know—no, I *believe*—that this is all necessary, that this is all deliberate, that my mom in some greater cosmic, karmic, Buddhist sense somehow left these clues for me. Kana, Laini, Sarah. Soon, Takahashi. That if I can figure them out, I can heal.

But if my mom were here now, I'd tell her that she has given me the best of her, but that she messed up on this one count. I'd tell her I could have managed. I would have wanted to know. I'd tell her that this is the part of her I don't want to be like. She may have had her reasons, and I think—now, *here*, after these weeks in Tokyo—I can respect that. But as for me, I will not be someone who harbors secrets, because secrets eat away at love.

Maybe this is what she wanted me to figure out. My own path.

I leave the cemetery because I have to be somewhere right now. Tonight is Kana's show. She's performing with her band. I texted her earlier to tell her. **Guess what? Holland showed up last night. And I also need the address of your show.**

I grab my phone to see if she sent me the address.

I WANT ALL THE DETAILS! Can't wait to see you at the Pink Zebra tonight!

There's an address and a time. Her show starts soon. I shift into high gear and hop onto a train. I must tease her about the name Pink Zebra. It sounds like a gay bar or a strip club. Once I'm in Roppongi, I find the Pink Zebra at the bottom of a hill, the far end of a slim alley, down a set of stairs, underground. There is no flashing sign to guide you, just a faded dark pink one with the name in curvy letters. I walk inside, and there she is onstage, blowing air into the sax, her cheeks like chipmunk cheeks, like Dizzy Gillespie on his trumpet. She is playing some jazz number I don't know. She wears a green sequined T-shirt, a jean miniskirt covered in ironed-on patches of brand names like Coca-Cola and Crest, and then rainbow knee-high socks inside a pair of pink Converse sneakers. Her sax is covered with stickers of pandas.

She plays with her eyes wide open, with her body moving, like she's giving life to the instrument, or maybe its notes are what give her so much life, so much zeal. She notices me at the end of her solo, and her eyes light up like sparklers set off on the Fourth of July. She is a beacon of light, a magnet; she is Tokyo itself, vibrant, twenty-four-seven, nonstop, and neon.

The song finishes, and she points to me and then bangs out a few notes from "The Stars and Stripes Forever." I laugh and point back at her as I sit down. I drink a Diet Coke the waitress brings me as I listen to the rest of their set, and when it's over, Kana jumps off the stage, sits down in my lap, wraps her arms around my neck, and stares at me with her big brown eyes. *"What did you think?"*

"You were amazing."

"I'm so glad you're here."

"Me too."

"So." She says it like a command as she gives me a pointed look.

"So?" I repeat back to her.

"So how did it go with Epic Superwoman last night?"

I give her the details. Her eyes grow wider and wider.

"And have you seen her today?"

I shake my head. Kana swats me, then scoots off my lap and into a chair next to me.

"Hey! That hurt!"

"Good. It should. You are madly in love with this girl, she flies to Tokyo to tell you everything, and you are here with me? You are an idiot who deserves to be swatted many, many times!"

I hold up my palms.

214

She puts her hands on her hips. "Go see her now."

I shake my head again. She peers at me, staring hard, and leans closer and closer as if she is burning a hole in me with her eyes.

"Kana. It's not that simple!"

"It *is* that simple."

"No."

"Yes."

"No."

"Yes."

"Okay. You win. Why is it that simple?"

"You love her, right?"

I shrug.

She waves a hand. "Allow me to answer this question. *Yes, Kana, I love her.* So move forward."

"How? She kind of kept a big secret from me. And she kind of broke my heart in the process."

Kana places her index finger next to her lips and looks at the ceiling. "I'm thinking. I'm thinking. Wait. Was she pregnant and didn't know if she was going to keep the baby when all this happened? And was your father gone and your mother getting sicker at this time?"

I roll my eyes.

"It's not easy being a teenage mom. Just ask my mom. The point is, my pigheaded, wonderful, amazing American friend, she had a lot going on too. Both of you did."

"Okay. So what of it?"

"Danny, you have every right to be hurt. And every right to shut her out and say good-bye to her forever. So I'm not saying what she did didn't hurt. But I *am* saying you can get over it. And more important, you *can* forgive."

"What if I don't want to?"

She reaches out a hand to ruffle my hair. "That is just all your walls talking. That is not your heart."

"And what does my heart say? Since you seem to think you know it so well."

She presses an ear against my chest. "Wait. I think I can hear it now." She pretends to listen again. "Oh yes, I totally agree." She jams her ear against me once more. "Definitely. That's what I think too!"

She pulls away.

"What did my heart say?"

"When you're ready, you'll listen to it, and you'll know."

I laugh. "You know what it's like hanging out with you?"

"It's like having someone call you on your BS all the time?" she asks with a kooky smile.

"Something like that."

"Go see her tomorrow."

"No. Tomorrow Takahashi is back. Kana, will you come with me tomorrow?"

"To Takahashi?" She looks bewildered by the request.

"Yes. I mean, not the meeting itself. But will you go with me to his office? Like how you took my mom to some of her appointments?"

"I would be honored," she says, and I'm glad I will have her company tomorrow. I'm glad I won't have to go alone.

Then she finishes my soda and plunks the glass down hard. "Now I have something to ask you."

"Anything."

"I want you to walk me home, and I want you to narrate."

"Narrate?"

She nods. "Yes. I want to see Tokyo through your eyes. I want you to tell me why you love it here."

It is the least I can do for her. To help her fall for the city where she's always lived. The city I've *always* loved.

We leave, and when we walk by a girl in the crosswalk whose heels fall out of her sky-high shoes with each step she takes, I say to Kana, "Welcome to the land of three sizes for shoes. Barely fits, hardly fits, and doesn't fit at all."

Then a nightclub with red flashing signs three stories high and techno music seeping through the doors. "Tokyo, the *real* city that never sleeps."

Next a pack of girls our age suddenly picks up the pace and runs toward a pink wooden stand on the corner selling bubble tea. " 'This just in. There is a bubble-tea shortage in Tokyo tonight. Sue, teenagers in Roppongi are reportedly hoarding bubble tea.' 'Bob, when was the last time this happened?' 'Well, Sue, it reminds me of the great bubble-tea shortage of 1989...' "

Kana laughs deeply, then we sidestep a too-cool-for-school guy, wearing a striped vest and variations-on-a-hipster jeans, so I slide into another riff, pretending I'm the hipster guy. " 'That girl in the rainbow socks totally wants me. She can't resist me in my skintight jeans even if I. Can't. Breathe. In. Them.' "

I walk Kana the rest of the way home, and when we're outside her building, I give her a hug, and she squeezes me tight. She holds on, and our bodies are close; we are connected in some way, and I feel something for her I haven't felt in a long time. But it's not a desire to touch her, to run my hands over her and press her against the wall, like I want to do with Holland. This may sound crazy or silly, but I feel like Kana is my sister too. Maybe she is the sister I was meant to have now. Maybe she is my second sister, for this fully orphaned phase of my life. Maybe a piece of Laini, the piece that shut me out long ago, has been reincarnated in Kana. Or maybe it's the piece of Laini that still cares that is now carried on in Kana.

And what I'm about to say to Kana has nothing to do with Jeremy or even Sandy Koufax. It is not meant to disrespect either of them or to knock them down. What I am about to say is this moment, this month, this summer. "This is going to sound totally crazy, but I kind of feel like you're my best friend, Kana."

"I totally think of you as my BFF too."

I believe *she* is why I was drawn to Tokyo. I believe somehow that my mom, wherever she is, brought me here so I could meet Kana Miyoshi. Because I know Kana is what I need and what I want.

For a second I feel something like joy.

I try to hold on to that feeling as I say good-bye and return to the Shibuya night.

Chapter Twenty-Four

Kana waits for me on the corner, sitting outside at a café, aimlessly kicking a ruby-red-slipper-clad foot back and forth as she nurses a slushy-looking drink. She peers at me over her big, round black sunglasses that I swear are half the size of her face. "Ready, Freddy?"

"Guess I'd better be."

We descend into the subway again. I know this station so well by now—passing through the turnstiles and hopping onto the train is like rote, like muscle memory. We board, and as the train slaloms through the tunnels of underground Tokyo, I know I have reached the last mile. Takahashi is the last stop, and whatever I learn from him will be the last thing there *is* to learn about my mom. Something about the visit feels ritualistic, like a rite of passage, maybe the way graduation should have felt.

"What do you think I should be ready for?"

"Whatever you might learn."

"Cryptic today, Kana?"

"I don't know. Maybe. I just know you've put a lot of stock in this visit with Takahashi."

"What do you think he'll say, O Wise One?"

"I think you already know."

"Do I?"

She nods, and her brown eyes remind me of my dog's. I stare into them for a few seconds. Her glasses are pushed up on her head; her black hair is like a waterfall of silk around her face. Her hair is down today, no ribbons, barrettes, or headbands.

Do I already know what he'll say? Do I already know what my mom wanted from the doctor who was her last great hope?

She would have asked him to help her live a few more months, of course. *Of course* that's what she would have said to him.

But then why would all those pill bottles still be full?

A dark fear rises up, but I push it back down. I shove it aside. Instead I remember something Kana said the first day we met at the teahouse, about how stories were her thing, about the way she seemed to sparkle when I told her the story of my neighbor's lilacs when we visited the temple.

"Do you want to hear a story?" I ask Kana, because maybe it's in the stories that the people we love are still alive.

She lights up and nods a big yes. I can give her this one, as she has given me so many.

"I used to play baseball in high school. Not like I was some major-league prospect or anything," I say as the train weaves around a corner and we lean with it. "But I was good, and I helped our team win a district championship in tenth grade. But at the end of my junior year, I blew out my shoulder."

Kana quirks up her eyebrows, waiting for me to explain.

"It wasn't bad. I mean, it *was* bad, because I'd torn my rotator cuff, and I couldn't play my senior year. I was bummed because you want to go out on top. I knew high school would be the last time I played ball, and I was going to miss all of my senior year. Which meant that baseball as I knew it was over. And my mom was awesome about it. She said all the right things and took me to this great ortho surgeon at UCLA to go over surgical options. But there was no point in going under the knife, since I wasn't going to try to play again. My shoulder healed on its own with time. So when the season started in February, and I wasn't on the field or with the team, my mom said we needed to honor the end of my baseball career and also celebrate my *new* life, without baseball. It was like paying homage to the sport, to what it had meant to me, she said. It would be a way to give thanks to baseball."

"Like baseball was a friend to you," Kana says.

"Yes, exactly." The train pulls into our stop, and we exit. I continue the story as we walk up the subway steps and into the Asakusa district, one of Tokyo's more traditional neighborhoods, with shrines and shops and less flash than the other places we go. "So we took Sandy Koufax to the baseball diamond where I played my first-ever game in this little neighborhood park in Venice Beach. I was nine then. I had pitched, and we'd won. And since my mom kept every little memento under the sun, she brought photos of me pitching and of the team celebrating after we'd won. And she even had my uniform and my hat from back then."

I shake my head at the memory, amazed at my mom's pack-rat tendencies when it came to this stuff.

"Did you put it on? The hat?" Kana asks, eager for more. Stories like this are Gatorade to her; they replenish her.

"It didn't fit, but I put on the hat just to be silly, I guess. I said, *I'm going to look incredibly stupid putting this on, but this one's for you, Mom.*"

Kana playfully punches me in the arm. "I bet she loved that."

"She did," I say as we walk past a store selling cookware and long steel knives. "She handed me a tennis ball and said we would honor that first game by pitching to Sandy Koufax. She told the dog to sit at home plate while I walked to the pitcher's mound. I went into my windup and threw to Sandy Koufax. She leaped up and caught it in her mouth. She was the true natural. Then she ran out to the pitcher's mound and dropped it in front of me and stared at it. That was her

223

way of saying, *More.* I lobbed a few more balls to her, and my mom and I just laughed. Then my mom said, *One thing passes into another. Now your arm serves that dog.*"

Kana beams, a bright, shining smile. "I like that. I like the idea of saying good-bye to one thing but welcoming another."

"Exactly. That's exactly what my mom was doing. She'd also gotten some bakery cake, and she brought plates and forks and a knife. So she sliced up pieces, and we sat down by home plate, and we ate cake and looked at pictures. And she let the dog have a piece of cake too. She joked that she'd make me a cake too for graduation," I say, adding the air quotes that my mom used at the time, making light of her baking—or nonbaking—abilities. I turn to Kana. "But that didn't happen. She always said she was holding on for graduation, Kana. She always said that. But she didn't make it." I choke up. That dark fear resurfaces, and I can't help but think that I already know the reason why she didn't hang on. Why she wanted to have that cake on the baseball diamond then. Why that day was the ceremony. Because I don't think her business advice from long ago was just business advice. Because one thing *does* pass into another.

"No. She didn't. But we are here now," she says, and gestures to a door, the same one I banged on more than three weeks ago. Takahashi's name is on it. "Call me later."

"I will."

Kana waves good-bye, then I ring the bell and wait for the doctor to let me in.

Chapter Twenty-Five

Takahashi is tall. Surprisingly tall. He is my height, six-two. I'm not used to Japanese people being the same height. I'm not used to most people being the same height. He wears a suit. A gray business suit. I guess, after the temple and the teahouse, I expected a short Zen master in some traditional Asian garb, maybe in a feng shui-ed, Zen-i-fied garden office.

Instead his office is like a European library, with oak furniture, an ornate navy-blue couch, and tall bookshelves lined with leather-bound editions of Japanese and English texts. Takahashi doesn't offer me tea, like I expect. Instead he opens a cupboard on his shelves and places a bowl of candy on the table between us. Bags of candy are inside the cupboard. He gestures to the crystal bowl in front of me. It is filled with lemon and orange sucking candy.

"Please. Take one," he says, and reaches for one, popping a lemon candy into his mouth. "I am a candy connoisseur," he says as he sits down across from me. I'm on the blue couch, and he sits in a deep, rich red chair. I feel like I'm at a shrink's. I've never been to a shrink's office, but I suspect it feels like this. Like feeling displaced. Like someone trying to make you feel comfortable. But the truth is, everything about being here is a Tilt-A-Whirl. Everything is off, different from what I pictured. My hands feel clammy, and I try to rub my palms against my shorts, but the clamminess is inside me. It's stuck in me, jammed in there like a too-stuffed drawer that won't close, squeezed along with everything else—with hope, with fear, with wanting, and most of all with *knowing* this is the end of the line. I want so much for him to tell me something I don't know, something that will make sense of my life, like my mom has been in his office all this time, the first case of an experimental procedure to cure cancer, and look: Here she is, all better now.

"Though truth be told, it's really an addiction. I can't stop myself when it comes to candy."

Is he really talking to me about candy? I take an orange one to be polite and put it in my pocket for later. My leg is shaking. I press my hand down on my thigh to quiet it. I think I'm supposed to speak first. "How was Tibet?"

"Uplifting," he says. "I treat the poor and indigent there who are suffering. They are grateful for the help."

"I imagine they are."

He sucks on the lemon candy, his cheek pouching out as he does. Should I ask him next if he's climbed Mount Everest? Because that's about all I know of Tibet—that the big peak is nearby. But I don't ask that. He doesn't go to Tibet to climb Mount Everest. I bet he goes there because it is part of his way of life, part of his beliefs.

"What do you do there? In Tibet?" I ask, because it is so much easier to say that than, *Did my mom stop taking her medicine?*

He tells me about his work there. I hear maybe every three words, and though I tell myself to focus, to listen, inside I'm scrambling to figure out how to ask what I most want to know.

"But I suspect that is not why you are here," he says gently, and I want to thank him profusely for putting me out of my small-talk misery.

"No. That's not why I'm here, Dr. Takahashi. You treated my mom," I say, stating the obvious, as if I can just ease into the difficult conversation.

He nods and begins to explain his credentials, his approach. But I know what he's written, I know the research he's done, the awards he's received.

"She thought of you as a medicine man, some kind of healer. Like a spiritual healer," I continue, starting smaller, circling the big question.

He nods. "I am flattered."

But I'm not here to flatter him. "Are you?"

"A spiritual healer?"

"Yes. You sent her to drink that tea. She thought it would heal her."

"She was looking for all sorts of healing," he says, and I'm tossed back to the afternoon at the teahouse, to Kana's words to me as well.

Sometimes healing isn't about our bodies.

"Do *you* believe in that legend, then? The one about the tea, about the emperor and his wife?"

"I believe that sometimes if you believe you are healthy, you are healthy."

"Mind over matter?"

"There is something to it, Danny. There is something to the energy in the universe, the energy you put out, the energy you take in."

"And does that work for cancer treatment? Or is that more for, say, nerves or headaches?" I ask, and I'm instantly embarrassed because I sound so sarcastic, so snippy. I didn't come here to accuse or to interrogate, but my old habits die hard.

But before I can apologize, he speaks again. Calm and gentle. Every word chosen with care, it seems.

"I am saying that if you have someone who wants to heal, sometimes they will respond to the unconventional. Their minds are more open to healing, so their bodies become more willing too. I believe that medication, while a wonderful thing, has its limits. That there are answers to be found in the unconventional. And she wanted that. She asked for that. I treated her with traditional cancer meds, and also with Chinese herbs and acupuncture, to minimize the effects of the chemo. I was in touch with her doctors in LA. As I'm sure you know, they were following this protocol too. And yes, I encouraged her to go to the teahouse and to see the temples and to keep her mind and her heart open to new ways of healing."

"She *was* open to healing. She was willing. And it still didn't work." I hold out my hands, waiting for an answer. "So why did she keep coming over here every month? When the cancer came back, why did *she* come back? What did she think was going to happen? She talked about you as a miracle doctor. She thought you were going to save her," I say, working hard to keep my voice measured now, to hold back all my darkest fears. My jaw is tight, I'm clenching my fists, and all my muscles are tense, but this time it's not because I'm angry. It's because I'm terrified of what he's going to say. I'm petrified of falling apart again. "And when my mom first saw you, she was great," I say slowly, doling out each word so I can keep it together. "She was doing better than in years. She was so sure she was going to be in the clear." I try to speak again, but the sounds in my mouth are a chasm, and I am at the edge. Somehow I manage to say, in the barest of whispers, "*I* was so sure you would save her. *I* wanted you to save her."

I wanted it more than anything. More than Holland, even.

I look at him, but it's not him anymore; he's twenty,

thirty, forty feet away, and everything is shrinking and expanding, and I don't think I can even see the walls in the room anymore. I'm cycling back over everything I hoped for. Everything I wished for in the last five years. My mom had been to Mexico, to the Mayo Clinic, to every doctor in Southern California, to Stanford, to Greece for some whacked-out treatment that didn't work. She was in and out of remission all the time. She wanted to live; she wanted to make it; she fought for so long. And then she found *him*.

The possibility of a miracle.

But he wasn't just my mom's last great hope. He was mine as well.

"If I could have saved her, I would have. I do everything I can to help my patients. That is not just my job. That is my calling." Takahashi presses his hands together and leans forward in his chair. "And your mother was one of the bravest, toughest, most resilient people I have ever known. She lived longer than anyone thought she would with her diagnosis. On paper, she should have died years ago."

The lump rises in my throat.

"But she was as strong as the cancer. She was stronger most of the time," he says.

"She could have lasted two more months then. Couldn't she have?" I ask as desperation gets the better of me, and my voice rises. "She wanted to. Don't you know how much she wanted to?" I push the question onto him, throwing it in his hands, and as I do I can hear the words echo—but

230

not just the words, the *idea* of the words, of what it means to want to hold on.

"She wanted to live, more than anyone I have ever treated. She had the strongest will to live. And that is why she lived so long. That is why she was as healthy as she was for someone who had cancer. I am sure you can recall that she was more well than she was not the last five years?"

I think of breakfasts at the fish market, of walks with Sandy Koufax, of crosswords she filled out, of songs she played on the piano, of the boat orchids she planted. She *was* more well than not. She was ridiculously healthy a lot of the time for someone who was so sick.

"Yes."

"But when she worsened, she knew her time was running out. And so, Danny, she wanted to heal in her own way, in the only way that she *could* heal at that point."

And so now I am here. The last thing. "So she stopped taking her meds?"

"Most of them, yes."

"Was she trying to break a habit or something?"

He shakes his head. "No. Not at all. She hadn't been dependent on pills or medications. She didn't feel beholden to them, but even so, she made a deliberate choice when her treatments ended to stop all medical assistance. She made a choice then to finish out her days as free as she could be. She wanted to experience life and death on her own terms."

"When you sent her to the teahouse, it wasn't because of

the legend then, right?" I ask, even though the question hurts as it forms in my throat.

He nods. "You are correct. I did not send her there for the legend of the tea. I did not send her there for the mystical powers of the Tatsuma tea."

I press my lips together, then speak. "You sent her there for some kind of peace, right? Peace of mind. That's the healing she was looking for?"

"Yes. Yes, I did. And yes, that's what she was looking for."

I know I have to ask the final question. I know *this* path is leading to *this* question. And I think I know the answer. It's come in and out of focus these last three weeks, and it's the thing I've been dreading. The answer I've always pushed aside. I can't push it aside anymore.

"She always told me she was holding on to see me graduate. That that's what she was fighting for and living for. She told me the reason she held off cancer for five years was to get to my graduation," I say, but as the words come out, I can feel, finally, how small they are, how hollow they are in light of everything my mom embraced, everything she was. Still, I need to come out on the other side. "But I don't think she was holding on anymore, was she?" I ask, but I know the answer. *I* was the one holding on then. *She* was the one ready to go. "She stopped holding on, didn't she?"

There is a pause, so quiet it's like his office is now the temple, so still I can smell incense drifting through.

"She told me she was ready," the doctor says. "She said

she was ready to die. That she did not want to hold on any longer."

For a second, I want to ask if it was suicide. If he's just another version of Dr. Kevorkian. But I don't. Because it wasn't, he's not, and she never would do that. Instead I say what I had feared to be true. What I now *know* to be true. Something I've denied and hid from but finally figured out before I walked in the door. Something I was terrified of moments ago. But something that I also know I can finally handle. "She came to you first for treatment, then for release."

He nods, the kind of sage nod of the wise man. "Yes. She was ready to move on. She came here to find peace, to be weaned off her meds in a way that was safe, so that she could die on her own terms. So that she could seek solace in the world around us." He gestures to the windows of his office, a gesture I understand to indicate the temples beyond. "To come to peace with the moving on. It is a gift, in a way. We spend so much of our time fighting death, as we should. But sometimes the greatest gift we can give ourselves, and in turn the ones we love, is to know when to let go. To know when it is time—and to be at peace with that."

Maybe he is a faith healer after all. Because it seems what my mom found in Tokyo, more than anything, was a new faith. Faith in the Buddhist ways; faith in the belief that everything happens as it should, in its own time, that we move on from one phase of life to the next, whether we celebrate it with a ceremony or not.

For her there was no more resistance, just readiness, just the letting go.

It hurts knowing that. But it also *doesn't* hurt like I thought it would. Because I finally understand. It was never really about the pills. It was never really about tea or treatments. It was about moving on.

I stand up and hold out my hand to shake Takahashi's. He was my mom's last great hope, and that's all I ever saw him as too. But now I understand who he is and what he was. Because now I finally have all the things I came to Tokyo for, all the things I didn't know about her:

That Takahashi was not only her last hope for life but her great hope for a peaceful death too.

Chapter Twenty-Six

I am outside, back on the street I walked down only an hour ago. It is just me now, me and this city, this adopted home that I have always loved, that I still love. Asakusa is not Shibuya. It is not neon and lights and flash. It is subtler: It is bamboo and temples; it is kimonos and sandals. It is a long shopping alley with open-fronted stores and carts and people weaving in and out as they hunt for seaweed and fish, for rice crackers and biscuit sticks dipped in chocolate. I find myself walking down this shopping arcade, part of the flow of people—the shopkeepers and the workers, the families walking through and the tourists scooping up folded fans and miniature red cat statues.

An older Japanese woman with graying hair and lines around her eyes nods at me as I walk past the display of *mochi* cakes she is selling. I stop, reach into my pocket for some yen, and buy a packet of *mochi* filled with strawberries. I eat one as I continue on, passing a small store peddling embroidered jackets, then souvenir shops selling tiny replicas of a nearby temple, Tokyo's oldest temple, built for the goddess of mercy. I've been to the temple itself, many times, on family trips.

But it's not the temple or the visits I remember now as I walk past men on bicycles with shopping bags in the metal baskets, past women pushing strollers, past all this regular, everyday life.

All this beautiful, wonderful, amazing everyday life.

I remember some of the last words my mom said to me. She was lying down on the living room couch, under a blanket, petting Sandy Koufax. "Obviously," she said, "I'm going to miss your graduation." Then she became serious but also content. "But in some ways it'll be like I'm there. I've already pictured it, imagined it, constructed it in my mind. And I've watched it. I've clapped, and I've cheered, and I've cried. And I am proud of you. Life is short, and life is beautiful, and everything is lovely. Love it, embrace it, smell the lilacs, play with the dog, and love endlessly and fiercely with everything you've got. Live without regret."

My mom's life was all it could be. She made sure of it. She made sure of it in the way she lived—and the way she loved.

Because there was no magic cure. There was no secret remedy, no ancient tincture to save her, to save anyone. But then there *was*. There *is* and always will be. The magic cure is in how she lived her life, and even more so in how she chose to die when given the choice. My mom, even in her death, has shown me yet again how to live and how to love.

That's the secret. That's the cure.

I am no longer the left behind. I am the living. And I want everything this life has to offer.

I stop for a second and look around at all the shops and stores and stalls. At all the people, going about their days, at all the moments they're living.

This is what I want.

I want to live every moment. I want to feel everything. I want to love one girl.

I want to walk down this street with Holland. I want to show her the stores, I want to take her to the fish market, I want to buy her rings and bracelets and all the silly things she loves, I want to share these *mochi* cakes with her, I want to introduce her to my new best friend, and I want to hang out with both of them. I want to be with Holland here, like we planned. So many nights ago, back in my house, in my bed, I wanted her to come find me. She didn't find me then, but she found me now, and we aren't the same people we were the first time or even a few weeks ago. We're different, but we can be different together. Because this is what *I* believe—that second chances are stronger than secrets. You can let secrets go. But a second chance? You don't let that pass you by.

I dial a familiar string of numbers and hit Send. She

answers on the second ring. She sounds nervous when she says my name. "Danny."

"Do you remember how my mom was always saying how she wanted to look back on her life and know she'd done everything she could?"

"Of course I remember that about her."

"How when she once took me out of school early to go surfing when I was in ninth grade, she said, *This will be one of the things we look back on at the end and are glad we did.* Even though neither one of us was very good at surfing. But it was eighty-two degrees and there wasn't a cloud in the sky, and she felt good that day, so we went and we caught a couple waves. And how she always ordered her lattes with low-fat milk rather than skim, saying, *I'm pretty sure I won't wish I'd had more nonfat lattes when it's all said and done.* And how much she traveled. She always said that when she got to the end of her life, she wouldn't regret a trip to Italy or Barcelona or Tokyo."

"That sounds exactly like your mom."

I look up at the sky. It's cloudless, like that day my mom and I played hooky at the ocean.

"Where are you right now?"

"I'm at the Imperial Palace. Well, outside. Walking around the gardens."

Of course. Holland. Gardens. They go together.

"Will you wait there for me? It'll take me twenty minutes to get there. I have to catch the subway."

"Of course I'll wait for you."

238

The most interminable minutes I've ever spent sludge by as I wait for the next train. I pace, like a caged animal, on the platform and peer down the tunnels. When the light from the next train appears, I want to reach out, stretch my arms all the way down, and yank the train closer. Finally it stops and the doors slide open. The train charges by a few stops, and minutes later I'm racing up the steps, taking them two by two, and then I run across the street seconds before the traffic light turns red, the cars and cabs just a few feet away from me.

The Imperial Palace looms in the distance. I speed through the late-morning crowds in the park that flanks the palace. Or, really, the park that flanks the moat that flanks the palace. I *get* why the emperor needs a moat; I'm totally down with keeping people out. But I don't need a moat anymore; I don't want one. I cross the park and find the path to the gardens. I run along the edge of the pond, avoiding the tourists snapping photos of the mossy trees and lush green bushes and languid water. On the far side of the pond are the cherry blossom trees, their bare branches reflected back in the pond.

I see her. She stands next to the water, lily pads floating nearby. She's talking to an older, heavyset couple, obvious tourists in matching Hawaiian shirts and white sneakers. She holds a camera and shows them a picture on the back of it. She gives the camera back to them, and they smile and thank her. They walk away, and she sees me and her face lights up. She wears a V-neck white T-shirt, jean shorts, flip-flops, a ton of silver bracelets, and her star ring. Her hair is summer blond, wavy again.

I walk closer, and she does the same, and I'm sure my heart is beating outside my body. I want to hold her tight, but there are things that need to be said first.

"I'm sorry I was such a dick the other night."

She shakes her head. "You weren't."

"Yes. I was."

"It's not like any of this is remotely normal. It's not like there aren't a million ways I could have done this better. Or told you better."

"Yeah, but you flew all the way over here, and I couldn't even talk to you."

"So talk to me now," she says in a shy, nervous voice. "If you want."

"I do. I do want that."

We walk to a bench under a shady tree a few feet away. Neither one of us says anything for a minute, and maybe that's because *us*—whatever we were, whatever we might be—is so fragile, or maybe it's something else. Maybe it's because we both know there's something that needs to be done and said.

"Do you have her pictures with you? Sarah's pictures?"

"Yes. Do you want to see them?"

"Yes." I am ready.

She unzips her shoulder bag, a black canvas thing, and takes out a manila envelope. The sky is crystal blue, and the sun beats down. But the air is cool under the tree; we're not baking in the midday heat here on this bench.

"Is this weird?" she asks. She looks so vulnerable here with me, far away from all her bearings, her internal clock still off by many hours.

"No," I reassure her. But it is weird. I brace myself as I watch her hands unfold the clasp. I don't know what to expect. Part of me expects the macabre, the morbid, even though she said the pictures are of Sarah alive. But I never knew her alive, so all I can think of is a dead baby. Holland opens a slim brown leather photo album. It's a small album, the kind that holds just a few photos.

She holds it open on her lap and points to the first picture. It's black-and-white, an ultrasound picture. I read the type on the white border—twenty-two weeks.

She turns the page. It's a close-up of her belly, round but not huge. "I was twenty-four weeks. I took it myself," she says with a shrug, like she's apologizing for the angle.

The next picture is Holland in a hospital chair holding a tiny little creature wrapped in a white baby blanket. Just the top of the baby's head is showing, a smattering of dark hair on her head. When I see her hair, I feel like the wind has been knocked out of me again. The picture is just like the one I found in my mom's room, but I'm looking at it in a new light now, looking at it and knowing exactly what it is. My kid. And my kid had my hair. "She has my hair." The words don't sound like they come from me.

"Yes, she did," Holland says, and touches the back of my hair lightly with her hand, like she's reminding herself, like the touch of my hair is reconnecting her. She returns her hand to the photo album and turns the page again. In the next photo, Holland is smiling. She looks exhausted, her hair a wild mess, but she's holding Sarah in her arms and the photographer has captured both faces—mother and daughter. Sarah is tiny, her eyes are closed, but she's all there, all the parts—lips and cheeks and ears and nose.

"She slept most of the time, but in this picture of her in the Isolette you can see her eyes," Holland says as she shows me one of the last photos. Sarah is surrounded by wires and tubes, but she's wide awake, with a crinkly forehead and bright gray eyes that stare into the camera. There are specks of blue around the edges of the gray.

"She was going to have blue eyes, wasn't she?"

Holland nods. "I think so."

"Like you."

"Yes. Like me. And brown hair like you."

Holland closes the photo album. I expect her to be crying, but she's not. She seems peaceful. She seems okay with all of this, with showing me the pictures, with talking about Sarah.

"So my brown-hair gene beat your recessive blond. But your recessive blue eyes beat my brown."

"Sounds like we'd call that a draw."

Then in a quieter voice, I say, "She was cute. She was beautiful."

"She was ours."

"I wonder what she would have been like," I say.

"I'm sure she would have been very sweet. And very funny, like you. Lots of jokes about Captain Wong's."

"And she would have been easy to talk to, like you."

"And kind and thoughtful. She would have been thoughtful," Holland continues, though I'm not so sure I've been anywhere close to thoughtful lately.

"And caring. The kind of person who remembered to trim the boat orchids."

"And she would have made all the boys crazy," Holland says playfully.

"And I'd have hated each and every one of those boys, and I wouldn't have let any of them near her."

"Of course. But you wouldn't have needed to worry. Because she'd only have eyes for the boy she'd loved since she was in grade school."

"Would she?" I take the photo album away from Holland and set it gently down on the bench. It's just us now.

"Yes. Just like her mom did."

"Is that what her mom did?" I trace a finger across her palm.

"Yes. She was a goner for this one boy. No one else ever stood a chance, because she fell for the boy next door a long, long time ago. Well, a few blocks away. But, still, it felt like next door."

"And what about the boy?"

"I hope," she begins, nerves creeping into her voice, and

what she says next becomes a question, "he would have been in love with her his whole life too?"

"Totally. Like a disease. One that gnawed away at his heart and turned him into ice."

"Oddly enough she still loves him, even though he keeps calling her a disease."

I touch her bracelets next, then run my fingers up her arm, savoring the feel of her warm skin. I reach a hand into her hair. She leans into my palm and closes her eyes. I trace her cheek with my thumb, her face, her beautiful, gorgeous, perfect face that I could touch and kiss my whole life.

My lips find hers. They are as soft as I remembered, and she tastes spectacular.

We pull apart for a second and look at each other, sharing crazy grins. Then she comes in for another one, putting her hands on my cheeks like I'm hers, like she's claiming me, and she kisses me, hard and deep and with an intensity that is out of this world, or maybe it is clearly *of* this world.

To kiss again like this—I think it's safe to say that I am totally, 100 percent a happy guy.

But even though I want to do so many things to her right now, I force myself to focus on something else.

A ceremony, a ritual.

"I have an idea," I say, and when I tell Holland, her eyes glisten, but she says yes.

Chapter Twenty-Seven

Holland waits in a shoe store down the street from my apartment. I don't let her come upstairs, because I know us. If we are alone behind a closed door, we won't leave. I walk over to the windowsill and take a smooth, flat rock the size of my palm from the base of one of the more Zen-like plants. I find a Sharpie, and I drop that and the rock into a plastic bag. Finally I grab the envelope with the lilac seeds that Holland sent my mom.

I close the door, find Holland, and hold her hand as we walk across Shibuya to the narrow alleys and side streets that lead to the Tatsuma Teahouse. The teahouse is closed today, and we can't go in anyway. Still, I tell Holland the story Kana told me. Well, the parts I remember.

"I love that. It's beautiful."

I nod. "It's a love story."

"I like love stories."

Then we're off to the subway. We fly down five flights of stairs to the lowest platform. The subway doors close quietly behind us. My hand is on her back, and I watch her looking at the posters of Japanese women writing novels on cell phones and pictures of Japanese men drinking energy drinks. I'm nervous again; it's only a subway. But it's *more* than a subway. It's a subway in Tokyo, and I want her to like it here. I want her to fall for this city. *My* city. Funny how I came to Tokyo to reconnect with my family, but I found something so much simpler, something I didn't even know I was looking for. But it's here, all around me: in the streets, in the shops, on the subways. My home.

We exit at the fish market and climb the stairs up to the food stalls. Some are closed since it's afternoon now, but *that food stall* is open, and Mike is working.

"Long day, dude?" I ask.

He nods wearily. "The usual?"

"I'll let the lady go first," I say, then turn to Holland. She orders tuna and rice, and I ask for the same. I tell her about my mom, how she came here every day when she was in Tokyo, and how we ate here together when I was with her.

Next we head across town to the temple. My mom's temple now—that's how I think of it at least. We go inside and nod in unison to the Buddha. "She used to come here too. I think this place gave her peace."

"I can see her here. I can definitely see her here."

We leave the temple and make our last stop. No subway this time. Just a short walk to the cemetery behind the temple.

I take the rock and the pen from the bag. On the rock I write a name: *Sarah St. James.*

I hand it to Holland. She writes two dates. Then she reaches inside her black bag and takes out a tiny piece of Sarah's baby blanket. It had been inside the manila envelope with the photos. I place the rock on the ground—a marker, a makeshift gravestone next to these other gravestones. Holland tucks the piece of the blanket underneath the rock.

Together we sprinkle lilac seeds around the rock. They won't grow; I know that. They won't rise up and turn into a lilac bush in a few years. For a lilac bush to grow, you have to plant it, water it, and all that stuff. But that's not what this is about.

I hold Holland's hand. She squeezes mine back. "I smell lilacs everywhere. And I don't mean from the seeds."

"I know," I say. "I smell them too."

"This is going to sound weird, but lilacs don't have a different season here in Japan?"

I shake my head. "Nope. But sometimes they're just everywhere. And that's just the way it goes."

As we walk away the scent of lilacs lingers in the air.

◆ ◆ ◆

We're back at my apartment, and as I hold the door for her, I feel like I've had too much caffeine, or like it's my birthday and all I want to do is open my presents. The door clinks shut, and seconds later we've made it to my bedroom, and I am laying her down on my white futon. I tell myself to slow down, to not rip off her clothes, to take my time because we have time. Besides, she looks so gorgeous here on my bed, and I want to drink her in.

"Can I take off your clothes?"

"Please take off my clothes," she says.

So I do, taking off her bracelets, her T-shirt, her shorts, and everything else. Her clothes are scattered across my futon, marking my bed. I always want her clothes on my bed. *Always*.

I stop to look at her. She is naked, and it's the most beautiful sight. I run a hand along the back of her leg, thrilled to touch her again, to be able to. Her body moves against my palm, and she gasps, a soft, lingering sigh. It's all so achingly familiar and so incredibly new at the same time.

"Can I kiss you?"

"Please kiss me, Danny."

I start at her ankle, and she shivers under my touch. I look up at her, and she looks down at me, and we lock eyes for a moment. Then she whispers, *Don't stop*, and I reacquaint myself with her knees and her thighs, her belly and her hips, and everything in between. She says my name over and over, and it's almost too much. But I am up to the task.

Then her cheeks are flushed, and she has this happy, woozy look on her face.

"Hi," she whispers.

"Hi."

"I missed that too."

"Happy to make up for all the lost time."

Before we go any further, I ask: "So should we double up or something this time? You know, just to be safe."

"I'm on the Pill again," she says, and I raise an eyebrow. "Not for *that*. The doctors put me on it afterward. To get everything back to normal. Ugh." She covers her eyes with her hands.

"Hey," I say, and gently take her hands off her eyes. "It's okay."

"I know. I just don't want you to think I'm on it for other reasons. I haven't been with anyone since you."

I grin in response, then kiss her eyelids. "Good."

"But yes, we should use a condom too."

I give her a goofy thumbs-up. "Double the protection, double the fun."

It's still amazing, or maybe it's even better because here we are again, and we can't seem to stop returning to each other. I don't want to stop, not with her, not ever. When it's over and we're lying next to each other, I'm not relaxed, though, because I half-expect her to leave, to dart out and never come back.

"Holland, please don't leave me again," I say.

"I won't run away again." Then softly, shyly, "I'm yours, Danny."

She reaches for my hand, clasps it in hers.

"Then promise me," I say. "Promise me if something

happens, like Sarah, that you'll tell me. That you'll give me the chance to figure things out with you. You don't have to be alone."

"I know that now. I do. And I won't leave you alone when things are hard for you, like I did before. I promise."

I want to bookmark this moment, capture it for the rest of my life. I know there are no guarantees, not in life, not in love. But I'll take what I can get; I'll take what I can *give*. Another chance.

Chapter Twenty-Eight

On Sundays during the spring and summer, Holland would go with my mom to the farmers' market. They brought their canvas bags and bought up cranberry-walnut breads, honey-kissed peaches, sun-ripened cherries, and flowers, gobs of flowers. They bought huge bouquets and little bouquets of whatever was in season. Holland would put her flowers in vases around her house; my mom would do the same at our house.

"It's like living in Amsterdam," my mom declared as she returned with orange tulips. It was just a few days after Holland and I had our first kiss. We weren't *out* yet; we weren't officially a couple.

"Tulips! Tulips everywhere. We're living in Holland," the girl named after the country added.

"We are turning this place into our own Netherlands," my mom quipped.

"We're like the Dutch!"

It was Kate's turn to chime in. "Clearly you two have been practicing your nicknames."

"And look, we picked up some zinnias to plant. They'll bloom in time for Labor Day," my mom said. "They'll be gorgeous."

My mom and Holland went to the backyard and began working in my mom's garden, digging and planting and getting their hands dirty. At one point I stood by the sliding-glass door and watched them. Holland was kneeling in the dirt, her hands in the soil. She looked up, noticed me, gave me a nod, and then a wink. I tipped my forehead back to her, a slight grin in return, then went back inside.

Later that day when Holland had returned to her home, my mom flopped down on the couch and said to me, "You are so busted, Danny. How long did you think it would take for me to figure out you're involved with Holland?"

She was the cat that had caught the mouse, and she was satisfied with the hunt.

"I don't know what you're talking about."

"Denial will get you nowhere," she teased. "Now fess up."

"Mom, don't be gross. I'm not going to tell you anything."

"Ah-ha! So there *is* something to tell! I knew it, I knew it."

I just shrugged and smiled—an admission. "What do

you want for dinner? Want me to make some sandwiches or something?"

"Sure," she said, and I brought her a plate with a turkey sandwich on wheat. "You couldn't have made a better choice."

"You like turkey that much, Mom?"

"You know what I'm talking about."

"I do. I do know what you're talking about."

I'm glad my mom approved of Holland. And right now I kind of want Kana to approve of Holland too. We're at an old-fashioned noodle shop in Shibuya having lunch. We sit at slatted wood tables and are surrounded by solo businessmen and businesswomen loudly slurping their noodles in approval.

Holland covers her mouth with her hand and tries to stifle a yawn.

"Did Danny tell you I have secret Asian cure for jet lag?" Kana says as the waiter brings our bowls of noodles. She says it in a thick Japanese accent, clearly making fun of herself.

"It's not jet lag," I say proudly.

Holland laughs, then points to me. "American boys. What can you do?"

"It's a good thing I knew he"—Kana points her thumb at me—"was head over heels in love with you from the start. Made it so much easier to keep my hands off him."

Holland smiles. "I'm sure he was terribly hard to resist."

"*The worst!* Every day it was like pulling arrows out of my heart," Kana says dramatically, then mimics the process of removing these arrows.

"Oh, ha-ha," I say, but I'm glad they like each other, because you never know with girls. You never know if one thinks the other is stepping on her territory. The thought of me being territory for either of them is laughable, but I like that each of these girls can stake a claim on me, a different one but still a claim.

When we finish the noodles, Kana asks if Holland has had the sponge cake yet. Holland says no.

"That is a sin. And it must be rectified. But there are other sins that must be righted first, beginning with those flip-flops you are wearing, Miss Holland." Kana turns to me and says, "Danny, we will meet you at the sponge-cake place in thirty minutes." Kana hooks her arm through Holland's and escorts her out of the restaurant.

I'm alone again, and there's something I need to do. Something I should have done long ago. I hoof it back to my apartment—*my* apartment, my *home*, it's easy to say now because *this* is where I live—and open my mom's medicine cabinet for the first time since the night I arrived. The pill bottles are still there. I take them all to the kitchen and dump the contents of each one into the trash can. It turns out that disposing of medicine isn't that complicated. I looked up the guidelines online. You're just supposed to mix up the pills with "undesirables" like coffee grinds or cat litter and then toss them out in the trash. I don't have litter or coffee grinds, but I think trash is kind of undesirable too. I'm about to tie up the bag when I think of another bottle I've forgotten. Only this one is mine. I go to the living room where I keep my painkillers. I look at the bottle longingly for a second, remembering the feelings, the way these pills took the pain away, the way they took me away. I'll miss the escape. Still, I dump the remaining ones in the trash and toss the bag in the incinerator in the building.

I resume my path to the sponge-cake café, and soon Holland and Kana join me. Holland is wearing rainbow socks up to her knees and a new pair of pink Converse sneakers. She looks totally adorable.

Kana holds out her arm as if she's presenting Holland, in her new duds, to me.

"You know what they say," Holland says. "When in Rome…"

The next few days race by. Holland stays with me the whole time. Sometimes we sleep in together, and sometimes we eat breakfast at the fish market. Then we walk through the gardens in the afternoons and we stroll through the shops and she buys bracelets and plastic sushi for her mom. One afternoon we meet Kana and give her the wigs that have finally arrived, and she immediately models the electric-blue one. Later that same day I call Jeremy and tell him that he can have the piano, that it's all his now, and he shouts a victorious *yes*. Then, as Holland and I walk through the side streets, getting lost in the maze of alleys and then getting found again, she asks when I'm going back to California. I stop and consider the thought. It's not the first time it's occurred to me. Because the thing is, I can't really picture returning to California. This is where I belong.

"I don't know, honestly. I like it here. And I think I know a way to get Sandy Koufax here too. For the rest of the summer. I thought I would stay at least until school starts."

She nods. "So you know that promise I made? Not to keep secrets from you?"

I brace myself. Not now. Not after all this.

"Well, this might be a good time to let you know that I started reaching out to schools in LA. To see about transferring."

"Really?" I don't bother to hide the massive grin.

"Yeah. *Really*. There are some good options for the fall for me. What do you think about that?"

I run a hand down her arm. "I think if you're *really* serious about going to school in LA, then you should spend a few more weeks here. With this boy you're into. And his dog."

"Well, you already had me at boy. But dog too? Doesn't get any better than that."

"Is that a yes?"

"It is always a yes."

A week later Sandy Koufax arrives by private jet, well-rested and ready to fetch tennis balls. I say thank you to Kate's Tokyo client for letting my dog hitch a ride over the Pacific in such style. Kate, ever the wizard, even made some calls so Sandy Koufax wouldn't have to be quarantined. My dog slobbers me with dog kisses and happy whines.

Holland and I take her for her first walk in Tokyo, and all the sights and sounds make her a little bit nutty, but I know what she wants. As Holland heads off to meet Kana for jelly crepes, I take Sandy Koufax to Yoyogi Park as the sun goes down. I toss her a ball, and she chases it, returning to our routine instinctively, like it was just yesterday when we last did this. She is the same; *this* girl is the same. I have spent so much of my life surrounded by women, by girls, and here I am with a new clan—some I've known my whole life, some just a few months. It's good to be here with this new family, a patchwork family, in this place where I belong.

But for now it's just me and my dog.

Sandy Koufax rushes back to me, drops the tennis ball, and waits for another throw. I oblige.

Acknowledgments

One of the most frequent questions a writer hears is "Where did you get your inspiration from?" Often, inspiration comes from many places and many people.

First and foremost, the heart behind *When You Were Here* was inspired by one of the most amazing and resilient people I have ever known—Sharon Schneider. I spent time with Sharon, but I also came to know her more through stories of her—the stories of her life that my mother-in-law, Barbara Major, shared with me. Sharon was Barbara's best friend and fought a long and valiant battle with cancer for many years. But even in spite of Sharon's illness, she remained so focused on life, on enjoying it, on sharing love and laughter with her children, and on showing them the world. Sharon, if you were here today, you'd be thrilled and not at all surprised to know that Jenny and Andy are wonderful, warm, funny, thoughtful, fabulous twentysomethings, and I am so grateful to count them as part of my big extended family. While the character of Elizabeth is entirely fictional, she was absolutely inspired by Sharon's life, spirit, and heart.

Thank you then, Jenny and Andy, for not balking when I said I was writing a novel inspired by your mom. You guys are truly awesome.

On the subject of inspiration, I have to thank my fantastic husband, Jeff, for the initial spark. I still remember that afternoon at the dog beach when we brainstormed the potential for this novel as Violet chased tennis balls in the waves.

This story was also inspired by Gayle Forman, one of the most talented writers I know. As soon as I finished her novel *Where She Went* (the first of what would become three reads so far of that fabulous book), I knew I had to write a book with a teenage boy as the narrator.

Of course, my own parents are part of the inspiration for any story in which family, and the importance of the connections between generations, plays so central a role. You guys have always encouraged me to pursue my dreams, you have always believed in me, and for that I am so grateful because here I am, living the dream.

My agent, Michelle Wolfson, deserves an entire acknowledgments section alone for her amazingness. She read this novel in twenty-four hours and fell in mad love with it, has read every draft, and has never ceased to be this book's biggest champion. Michelle, you were my dream agent, and you became my actual agent, and you have remained a dream agent. I've said it to you many times, but it bears repeating—having you guiding my writing career has freed me to just write, and that is the greatest thing I could ask for as a writer. To many years of mind melds.

My editor, Kate Sullivan, continues to astound me with her razor-sharp insight and brilliance. She has known what this book needed every step of the way, and she has gently guided me into finding the heart of the story, and to taking off at least one accessory. Kate, your edits are challenging, mind-bending, and daring, and working with you to shape this story into what it has become is *why* I wanted to keep working with you. What a lucky writer I am to have you in my court. Let's do it again!

A big thanks as well to the team at Little, Brown that has shepherded this novel from its earliest stages, including Leslie Shumate, Victoria Stapleton, Lisa Moraleda, and Alvina Ling.

Many writer friends chimed in with valuable feedback along the way. Kody Keplinger looked at the first chapter way back when and gave me helpful input. Cynthia Omololu read many, many drafts and gamely participated in many more brainstorming and *what-if* scenarios. Cynthia—your smart and thoughtful feedback but, most important, your willingness to always be there as my go-to gal is so greatly appreciated. Courtney Summers cheered me on during the epic writing binge of this book—first draft in twenty-one days, thank you very much. More important, though, she read a draft during the final stages of editing and offered great insight on tweaking the characters and certain elements of the story to make it sharper and better. My local writer friends cheered me on as well—Cheryl Herbsman and Malinda Lo, I'm talking about you! Stephanie Perkins and Kiersten White—you're as fabulous as ever; I love our Wednesday "chats." Suzanne Young—you are adored.

As always, my best friend in the entire world, Theresa Shaw, was *and* is there for me, for every book, for every event, for every moment in my writing career. Theresa—you are inimitable, and I can't imagine navigating the insanity and the magic without you.

I am indebted to many online resources for information about doctor-patient confidentiality as well as health and medical guidelines in Japan. That includes a study on disease and prognosis disclosure conducted by the University of Tokyo, a study on ethical decision-making and patient autonomy in Japan and the United States conducted by the Stanford University School of Medicine, studies on patient autonomy and diagnosis disclosure conducted by the Department of Geriatric Medicine at Tan Tock Seng Hospital in Singapore, as well as the article "Comparison of Diagnostic Disclosure in Japan and the United States: From Communicative Perspective" by Tomoka Noguchi. I am also grateful for the insight from my doctor friends Sandeep Wadhwa and Louise Lo on doctor-patient relationships and how they impact the next of kin.

I relied on several sources for the Japanese translations in this novel. Thank you to Eric Sandler, Eve Eschenbacher, and Kana Kozawa, whose name also provided the inspiration for a central character in the novel. Any mistakes in Japanese are entirely mine.

Big thanks to Kathy Brooks for helping me understand more about the Jewish approach to the afterlife, and to Garry Brooks for his invaluable input on air-conditioning. Trust me when I say that both of your respective contributions on religion and on handyman-ism are equally vital!

Many thanks for the booksellers, teachers, librarians, bloggers, and fellow authors who spread word of mouth and, of course, to readers. I adore hearing from you. You, readers, are why I write.

Thanks to Cammi Bell, Ilene Braff, Kelli Anderson, and so many of my "real life" friends who were there when I got to say, "My book sold!"

I thanked my husband at the beginning of these acknowledgments, but I'll thank him again, because he makes the best sandwiches, finds the funniest TV shows, and always knows when I need a crazy cat photo or penguin gummies to pick me up.

To my children, whom I love fiercely and endlessly and with everything I've got. You guys are my loves. Always and forever.

And a tradition is a tradition is a tradition. Danny is fortunate to have a dog who is "the definition of perfect," because his dog *is* my dog. Violet, I am sure, would be delighted to lend her personality and looks to Danny's dog, Sandy Kou-fax, if she cared about such things. Alas, Violet cares most about tennis balls, kibble, and taking up as much space on the bed as she possibly can, since she is a bona fide furniture dog and will always have full furniture privileges, as all dogs should.

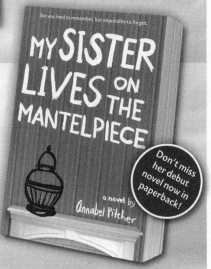
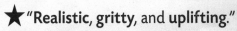

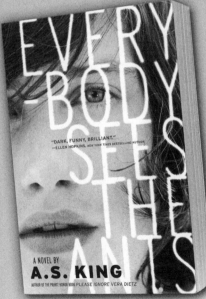
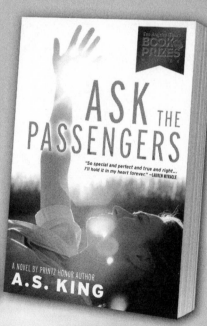

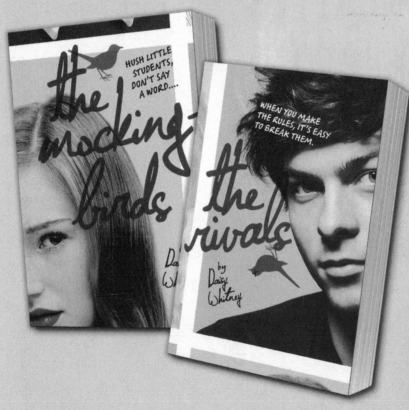